ONE NIGHT STAND

O'GALLAGHER NIGHTS

CONOR  MIA

MIGNON MYKEL

Also By Mignon Mykel

LOVE IN ALL PLACES series
full series reading order

Interference **(Prescott Family)**
O'Gallagher Nights: The Complete Series
Troublemaker **(Prescott Family)***
Saving Grace **(Loving Meadows)**
Breakaway **(Prescott Family)***
Altercation **(Prescott Family)***
27: Dropping the Gloves **(Enforcers of San Diego)**
32: Refuse to Lose **(Enforcers of San Diego)**
Holding **(Prescott Family)***
A Holiday for the Books **(Prescott Family)**
25: Angels and Assists **(Enforcers of San Diego)**
From the Beginning **(Prescott Family)**

* *The Playmaker Duet (Troublemaker, Breakaway, Altercation, Holding)*
can be enjoyed in one easy boxed set.

ONE NIGHT STAND

O'GALLAGHER NIGHTS

CONOR ~ MIA

MIGNON MYKEL

ISBN: 1540557065
ISBN-13: 9781540557063

Cover Design and Formatting: oh so Novel
Editor: Jenn Wood
All images and vectors have been purchased

O'GALLAGHER NIGHTS SERIES

One Night Stand
About Last Night
All Night Long
Hot Holiday Nights: Rory and Emily

NOTE FROM THE AUTHOR

Brenna and Conor O'Gallagher, specifically, have been playing around in my mind for a number of years but as a person who loves inter-connected series, I wasn't entirely sure how I could bring O'Gallaghers to life. In my head, they were a Boston-based pub and the Prescotts are a California/Wisconsin family, and another series in the future is Montana based (but still connected to those Prescotts).

But then one day Caleb Prescott walked into O'Gallaghers.

I wanted to try my hand in the erotic romance scene. I am definitely an in-your-head, let's-talk-feelings kind of writer so making a relationship happen because of sex rather than just thoughts and everyday actions was a challenge I wanted to give myself.

Conor was certainly fun to write, and I love Mia as she is. Not every virgin is this timid thing, and I wanted Mia to show the world that.

I hope you enjoy this little novella series, and if you are a fan of the Prescotts and Caleb, you'll get a little taste of him in here, too.

Welcome back to San Diego, and I hope you enjoy your visit with the O'Gallagher siblings!

To Mothers.
Just not mine.
She's not allowed to read this series.

PROLOGUE

MID-MARCH

O'Gallaghers was the place to go if you were looking for a good time. The local sport teams hung out there after games, for one, but also because the O'Gallagher siblings were a sight to behold.

At least, in my opinion.

I grew up with the siblings, once upon a time. From the time I could walk and all throughout high school, my parents and I lived next door to the O'Gallagher family. Brenna, the youngest of the trio, and I had been best friends up until the fifth grade. Conor, the oldest, and Rory, three years younger than him, were wild, flaunted sex appeal like nobody's business, and were *fiercely* protective of their baby sister.

They also didn't seem to think she was every bit as wild and crazy as they were, which was actually part of the breaking point in our friendship. By the age of ten, I was no longer good enough for Brenna.

While I remained the quiet, timid Mia, the only part that was wild and crazy about me was the brown, curly locks on my head. Two years after our friendship ended, I still held on to my baby fat while Brenna was the first in our grade to get breasts, then her period. She was the first to grow tall in our class, too. Sure, we eventually all caught up and she became the shortest in our grade, but it didn't stop the boys from noticing her. She was a five-four, C-cup beauty with raven black hair and piercing green eyes, and we were only twelve years old.

By fourteen, rumor had it she lost her virginity in the back of a high school senior's van. A classmate of Rory's, no less.

By sixteen, the rumors started circling she was pregnant.

She wasn't, I don't think, but it was a popular story, told again and again.

The thing with the rumors was that the people spreading them, the people responsible for them, were extremely careful to keep their words clear of Conor and Rory.

Brenna left for school in her conservative clothes and always returned home in them. She left clean-faced and was sure to wipe the make-up off before heading home.

I'm sure her brothers weren't stupid, but with everything else going on in their lives—senior year, college, and the like—if Brenna showed up clean and fresh and like the angel they thought she was, they could go on and pretend the same.

I never spread the rumors.

It wasn't that I was afraid of her brothers; quite the opposite, actually. At all of eight years old, I had fancied myself in love with fifteen-year old, Conor. He shared the same jet-black hair Brenna had, but his eyes were the type of blue you could see from a mile away.

So incredibly brilliant.

As much as I missed Brenna's friendship, it was the easy smiles her brother always had for us that I missed the most.

I sat at a high-top table in O'Gallaghers, my eyes on the man running the bar, hoping to catch that blue brilliance, willing it to aim my way.

Conor O'Gallagher.

I hadn't seen him in fifteen years so I doubted he would recognize me.

But I certainly recognized him.

Gone was the lanky, tall, clean-faced kid from our youth. In his place was a taller, broader man with a short, yet thick, beard. The only time he flashed his smile was when he was flirting and he always paired it with a sexy wink. Tonight though, was ladies' night, which meant he brought the charm up one-hundred-fold.

The O'Gallagher siblings were second generation Irish-Americans; their grandparents were from Northern Ireland. Anyone with any knowledge of Irish history would know that the Irish didn't wear kilts, but rather tunic things called lein-croichs.

Ok, maybe I looked it up.

But I had been pretty sure kilts were a Scottish thing.

Anyhow.

Thursday was ladies' night, and Conor and Rory brought it up a notch by wearing solid black kilts—last week's was saffron colored—paired with the forest green shirt that was part of the bar's uniform. No other bartender did the same, just the O'Gallagher boys.

They also both wore tan work boots, which should have made the ensemble ridiculous but rather...

It was fucking sexy as all get out.

I had been coming in a few times a week for the last three weeks, trying to get the nerve to go up to Conor. Re-introduce myself. See if he wanted to sit and talk, ease him into what I really wanted from him. Yet, every time I came in, I sat at this table, away from the bar and away from Conor.

I licked the corner of my lips as I lifted the glass of Irish ale to my lips, my eyes still on the man of the hour.

Each time I was there, I was helped by one of the female barmaids. If I wanted to be helped by Conor, if I wanted him to truly notice me, I would have to sit at the bar but I still had to form a plan because I wanted more than to just sit and talk and catch up.

You see, for all of Conor's flirting, he always backed it up. Sure, he flirted with damn near every female in the place, but if he gave you extra special attention, you just knew where your night was going.

Allegedly at bar close, he took one of the remaining ladies up to his apartment for a wild rendezvous. Never a virgin; he wasn't quiet about his lack of desire to take a virgin to bed. He liked the wild women who knew their own way around the bedroom.

Thursdays, rumor had it, he brought two up with him.

I didn't want to be one of two tonight, no.

But I did want one night with him.

A night to learn the ropes of sex.

Because if anyone knew what he was doing, it was Conor O'Gallagher.

And I was going to be his first virgin.

CHAPTER ONE

CONOR

I set the mixed fruity drink in front of the sexy blonde sitting at my bar and gave her a wink. Her drink choice needed work, but she would probably still be fun in bed.

Maybe she'd stick around for bar close.

I wiped my hands on the bar towel hanging from my belt and glanced up as one of my regulars-turned-good-friends came up to the bar, pounding on it twice with his fists, a huge grin on his face. "Yo, Conor."

I chuckled and nodded upward, working on a drink order one of my barmaids brought up. "What's up, Cael?"

Caleb Prescott was one of my regulars, yes. He played hockey for the city's NHL team and often came in with his brother or the team as a whole. He and I would sit and shoot the shit sometimes and I grew to like the guy. He was younger than me, but he was a good guy.

"I talked Syd into a date for the wedding." Caleb moved to sit in what had to be the only open stool at my bar and leaned forward on his arms. Caleb met Sydney during a dating show.

I take that back. Sydney was the casting person, and Caleb fell for her, hook, line, and sinker.

"She finally decided she was going through with it, hey?" I grinned and slid the glasses I'd filled over to the end to be picked up. "Your mug is good enough for her?"

Caleb grinned wide. "Fuck you, Conor. But yes, we decided on a date. And I want you to be there."

I stopped wiping my hands on my towel. Caleb and I were friends, yeah, but I didn't realize we were invite-you-to-the-wedding kind of friends.

"It's cool if you don't want to, or can't come. We're having it back in Wisconsin. But you're one of my few friends here that isn't on the team and Sydney likes you, so."

"Nah, yeah, absolutely," I said, reaching up to flip my baseball cap backward. "I'd be honored to go. Thanks for the invitation."

"I only asked because of Sydney," Caleb said with a grin.

"Yeah, whatever, fucker. You love me."

Caleb shot me the bird before standing to pull an envelope from his back pocket. "Don't tell her I gave it to you bent to shit, though. She spent a lot of time on them."

I laughed and shook my head. The guy was whipped. I couldn't imagine one pussy for the rest of my life, but hey, if he was happy...

I reached for the envelope and put it back by the register and legal pad, which I would have to take back to my office before the night was over.

"You want a beer?" I asked as I turned.

Caleb shook his head as he pushed back from the wood. "Nah. Chief made dinner and we have a game tomorrow, so I need to pass. See you tomorrow though? You get those tickets?"

I nodded, holding my finger up to a pretty girl waving in my direction. "I did. Rory was fucking ecstatic. They're great seats, thanks." Rory's birthday was coming up and Caleb hooked me up with tickets to the Enforcers-Wild game the next night.

"Absolutely. Happy to help. Talk later," Caleb said, holding his hand up in the air in salutation as he turned to leave. I shook my head, grinning, and went back to work, heading down the bar to the girl who flagged me down.

"What do you have on under that kilt, Conor?" she asked. She was certainly hot, with her dark hair and grey eyes, and her most definitely enhanced chest. Maybe she'd be willing to play tonight. Her blonde friend beside her was pretty easy on the eyes, too. Maybe she'd be up for some play time as well.

I chuckled and lifted a brow. "Wouldn't you like to know."

Everyone with a true Irish bone in their body knew that

kilts were a Scottish thing, and the kilts worn by the Irish were typically an American thing. When my brother Rory and I were trying to find ways to keep the bar from falling under the red line, we decided to go with the kilt idea. It didn't matter that kilts weren't a true part of our heritage, regardless of the Gaelic ancestry we had; we were Irish, and Irish-Americans liked to wear them.

That, and the ladies seemed to fawn over them.

So we wore them on Thursdays, which quickly became our best night of the week.

For the business and the bedroom.

I wasn't exactly private about my affairs. Many a drunk woman would stick around until bar close, hoping I'd pick them in my nightly game of eenie, meenie, miney, 'ho.

Some of those ladies were disappointed to learn that I wore boxers underneath, but only dimwits went bare under a kilt.

That and the phrase was "True Scot" and, like I said, I was Irish.

I walked down the bar to pour a lager that was ordered up from the floor when I could feel someone staring at me.

On my search for the stare, my eyes settled on the woman who had been coming into my bar a few nights a week for the last number of weeks. She sat at a high-top a few tables back from the bar. I'm not sure what snagged my attention, to be honest. She wasn't striking like the half dressed women who sat at my bar. No, she wore little makeup on her face and had a crazy mass of curls that looked like she fought to put back in the bun behind her head.

She never came in with anyone, never met up with anyone. It was only just ever her, sitting at one of my high tops, nursing some lager or another. I idly wondered what her story was, and what kept bringing her in. The bar had regulars, don't get me wrong, but she just didn't strike me as such.

When her eyes shifted and met mine over the bar and a couple tables, she quickly looked down.

Ah, so *she* had been spying on me.

She didn't look the adventurous type, but I had been surprised by women before. Maybe she wanted in on my fun tonight.

Sometimes it was the quiet ones that turned out to be the freaky-in-bed ones.

Knowing her drink, I poured her another and set it with the lager that had been ordered. When Emily, the quiet but beautiful barmaid we hired last week, came back for the lager, I pushed the extra glass toward her. "High-top four."

"Sure, Con," she said with a small smile. I watched as she delivered it, my hands slowly wiping and bunching at the towel at my hip.

When Emily sat the glass down, Curly Locks looked up, wide eyed. I couldn't hear whatever Emily told her, but before Emily left the table, Curly's eyes met mine again. I offered her a wink then went back to manning my bar.

One of my bartenders, Greyson Stone, walked behind the bar from the swinging kitchen doors. Yeah, his parents were fuckers for naming him that. "Hey, bossman."

"What's up, Stone?" We clasped hands and pulled into one another, bumping chests with our hands between us. Typical greeting.

Stone came to work for Rory and I three years prior, when O'Gallaghers re-opened for business. I needed a trustworthy bartender and while I hadn't known Stone from Adam at the time, he'd proven to be one of my best employees and a pretty damn good friend. That, and he didn't hit on my sister.

I filled orders as I talked to the man who wasn't supposed to be working tonight.

"What brings you in tonight?"

"Ah, Rory asked me to cover his last hour." Stone began going through coolers and chests, making sure all the fridges and condiments were how he liked them. The man was slightly OCD about it.

"What the fuck is Rory doing?" I glanced over at Stone, my peripheral on the lager I was pouring.

"Something about a girl," Stone said around a chuckle. He

grabbed a towel and hooked it into the back pocket of his cargo shorts.

I shook my head. Everyone knew I'd take a woman home at the end of the night, just like everyone knew Rory wasn't above taking one home in the middle of his shift. "Always a girl."

"You take a break lately?" Stone asked before his attention was snagged by a customer at the far end.

We split the bar, each taking a side, as the night hit a busy spurt. Thirty minutes later, the rush ended for the moment, and I remembered Curly Locks. I looked toward her table, sure she would have left by now.

But nope, she was still there, nursing the glass I had Emily send over.

"Stone, I'm going to take that break," I said over my shoulder. I grabbed two bottles of water and, carrying them in one hand, made my way out from behind the bar. I tossed my towel on the back counter by the register just before clearing the bar.

"Hey, Conor."

"Conor, my man, how's the night?"

Everyone knew who my brother and I were. Not only had we grown up in this town, but O'Gallaghers had been a prime establishment since our parents opened the doors twenty years ago. Five years ago, the doors closed when our parents decided to do the empty nester thing, traveling around the country in a fucking RV of all things. When I mentioned wanting to take over, I refused to accept the bar as a gift. They went on and on about how it was us kids' namesake and I should be willing to just take it, but I wanted to give them a sensible down payment. Between Rory and I, we accomplished that in just about a year, and roughly eighteen months after the doors closed, we re-opened.

The patrons who came on Thursdays were generally the younger crowd. And the ladies, of course. I would say that on any given night, I knew at least half of our patrons from school or around town.

I made general small talk with customers, some I knew,

some I didn't, on my short journey toward my destination.

The entire time, my eyes were on Curly Locks. She knew I was coming for her.

There may have been loud conversation and music playing all around me, but the only thing I could hear was my breathing and the slight thump of my Timberland work boots.

The closer I got to her, the wider her eyes became.

Trapped, baby.

I've got you trapped.

MIA

When Conor first caught me staring at him, I battled the need to leave. But then he sent the pretty waitress over with another drink. It was rude for me to leave then, even if I knew I wouldn't drink it.

I had a limit, and I was pretty strict about it. I had to drive.

When the bar got crazy busy, I almost slipped out then. I wanted to be unnoticed. I wasn't ready to 'meet' Conor. I had to come up with a plan!

Unfortunately, I found myself glued to my chair and when Conor's eyes found mine yet again when the crowd dwindled...

I had been frozen to the spot, unsure of what to do.

He stalked his way toward me now, black kilt hardly moving around his legs. My eyes traveled down, taking in his hairy but muscular calves, ending in short socks and tan boots. I brought my eyes back up to lock on his and sat up a little straighter.

Did he recognize me? Did he know who I was?

He finally reached my table and put a bottle of water down in front of me. "Your lager is probably warm and undrinkable by now."

His voice had deepened more in the last fifteen years. I mean, I knew it was going to happen. It had started well before the last summer I spent with his sister. But it was low and gritty, and it alone had my heart pounding behind my breasts and my pussy getting wet.

I licked my bottom lip before bringing it in my mouth to bite gently. I watched as his eyes focused on the movement.

I hadn't been intending on the highly sexual movement to be anything more than a reflex of my nerves, but the way his nostrils flared and his pupils dilated... Shit.

"You like what you see, Curly Locks?" His eyes slowly moved from my lips to my eyes.

So he didn't know me.

I wasn't sure if I should be relieved or embarrassed.

"I do." My voice held a huskiness I wasn't aware I was capable of.

"What are you doing tonight?"

Oh my God. This was happening.

I hadn't properly planned and wasn't expecting anything to happen tonight but oh my God.

It was happening.

I shifted in my seat and tilted my head to the side. I guess I was going to have to play it by ear. With a mental shake and a deep breath, I brought out my best bravado. "Nothing."

"I bet I could turn your nothing into a great night."

He leaned into the table, his forearms resting on the wooden top and he lazily slid his bottle of water from hand to hand, as if he didn't have a care in the world.

Well, he probably didn't.

He could have his share of women in this bar.

"I don't do threesomes." I lifted my brows in challenge.

"Ah, so you've heard about the *other* Thursday night special." He chuckled, one side of his lips lifting with the movement. "I can work with that. You see, Curly, I've seen you here in my bar, by yourself, a few times now. And I've felt your stare. I think you want to go upstairs with me."

There were so many things my mind wanted my mouth to spit out.

You know me.

How are your parents?

What has Brenna been up to?

I'm really damn proud of you and Rory.

YOU KNOW ME!

But I fought to keep those words back. Instead, I focused on his intense gaze and ignored my heart battling in my chest. "So what if I do?"

He winked and pushed away from the table before uncapping his water and taking a long, long drink from it. My eyes watched as his Adam's apple bobbed with each gulp. When he put the bottle back down, it was more than half gone.

"Stay put and I'll make your wildest dreams come true." He recapped the bottle and walked back to the bar much in the same fashion he had when coming toward me.

Proud. Confident.

Cocky.

Damn, I couldn't wait.

CHAPTER TWO

CONOR

I had been damn near positive Curly would leave in the hours between our chat and close, but nope. She sat at her high top, one leg crossed over the other, nursing the bottle of water I left with her. Sometimes she'd lean against the table, others she'd sit up straight. But always, her eyes were on me and my movements.

I knew what women like her saw when they watched me.

A man whom she considered was just out of her league. A man who would never take a moment to appreciate the plain shirt and jean-clad legs, hair in a mess of a bun, while women with perfect hair and perfect faces and perfect tits falling out of their hardly-there shirts leaned over my bar.

But pussy was pussy. Tits were tits.

And every now and then, it was fun to throw something different in the mix.

I glanced over my shoulder at the clock before turning back to the last of the bar's customers. "Closing time, ladies." As was usual, I was the last to be in the bar. My cooks left at eleven; the last of the barmaids left an hour ago, and Stone left an hour before that.

"What are you up to tonight, Conor?" a fucking gorgeous brunette asked me. Her eyes met mine, but not before checking out my junk.

Not that she could see much of anything under the heavy fabric of this kilt.

I was up, all right, but it wasn't for this brunette. It was for the one who kept her heavy gaze in my direction, who kept licking her fucking pink, full lips. Kept drawing in that lower lip.

Kept squeezing her fucking knees together as she sat with her legs crossed.

She was just as impatient as I was.

Most of the women generally were.

The brunette at the bar leaned over as she pushed her glass forward, a twenty under it. Assuming it was to cover her tab, I took the bill and turned to close her out. When I returned with her change, she winked. "You keep it. But tell me, Con. How much does a girl gotta pay for you to take her virginity?"

There was no fucking way this woman was a virgin. Not with how provocatively she dressed nor how strong she was coming on.

Her girlfriend beside her giggled into her hand. Either she was a happy kind of gal, or she had one drink too many. Considering I always watched out for my customers and their limits, I would say she was a happy girl.

"I don't fuck virgins, sweetheart."

I reached over with my towel to wipe down the bar beside these two. My rule against virgins wasn't anything bred from a terrible past or knowledge of horror stories of the whole *deflowering* process.

Nope.

Actually, I just didn't think it was fair to the woman.

I wasn't there to coddle, I wasn't there to make sweet love. I wanted to throw the woman down on the bed, rip her out of her clothes, and enter her without the preamble of foreplay and being sure she was ready. They were always mostly ready, some tighter than others, but always thick and hot and welcoming.

The pain, the tears, the *blood*; yeah, no thank you.

"Well, that's too bad, sugar," the girl said, pushing the change I just left her toward my end of the bar. "I'll just have to come back. Have a good night, Conor O'Gallagher."

The women left, leaving only Curly Locks in the establishment. I flicked my towel over my shoulder and rounded the bar, grabbing my legal pad and Cael's invitation on the way. I continued to walk toward the door, but addressed her. "You're still game?"

I looked over my shoulder, sure she would nod her response, and was pleasantly surprised to find she now stood near me. She smiled up at me and nodded. "Still game."

Looking down at her, I couldn't help but feel that I knew who she was.

It was in her eyes.

She looked strong yet slightly wary, a look I'm sure I'd seen a thousand times before. Maybe that was why.

"Alright then." I locked the front door and flipped a switch, turning off the neon advertisements and the "Open" sign.

I couldn't help but want to take her hand, but that wasn't me.

So I walked ahead of her. "Follow me then, Curly."

MIA

I nibbled on my lower lip as I followed him.

Fuck, I was nervous.

The entire time between now and when he had left me at the table with just a bottle of water, I thought about what would be happening tonight.

I wasn't a stranger to sex, per se. I had toys. I knew my body and was comfortable with it. Sure I was a little on the bigger side; my yearly biometric screening labeled me as "over-weight" even though I was about twenty-three percent body fat. I spent many years as a child battling my weight and finally as an adult, found a way to shed most of it. These days, I had muscle and was toned, but the pudge in my tummy and the extra under my chin when I tilted my head down... they bothered me.

But I fought hard for my body and I was fucking proud of it.

So yes, I was comfortable with my body and knew what got me off. At least, what got me off by my own hands.

I had vibrators, dildos, and this fancy little toy that sucked and pulsed around my clit. But the actual penetration from a real, live penis was what was new to me, and I couldn't help but be a little fearful for it.

Tonight though... Tonight was my ultimate dream come true.

I followed behind Conor as he walked toward the other end of the bar, flipping off the last of the lights. He pushed through the kitchen swinging door, hardly even holding it for me but for the tips of his fingers as he continued on through the kitchen.

I slipped through before the door swung closed on my face.

He obviously didn't bother with sweetness or gentlemanly acts. Was this all part of his show? To scare away the girl who wanted that sweet gentleman? He wasn't going to scare me away though. Nope.

I quickened my step so I was closer to him, but only in fear that I would truly end up hit in the face by a door. At the end of the kitchen, he turned a corner and reached into a room to flip off the light. Before he pulled the door closed, I recognized the room as an office.

Still, I followed him until we reached the end of this back room. After locking one more door, he opened up the last of them and reached into the hall the door led to. He flipped on a light in the hall before turning off the light to the room we just cleared.

Up the stairs we went, to what I assumed would be his apartment.

Great observation skills on my part, you know.

He opened the unlocked door at the top of the stairs. This time he waited for me. He stood against the open door, his back propping it open and his muscled forearms crossed over his chest.

"You change your mind yet, Curly Locks?" His eyes were challenging me.

I cleared the last of the steps and, chin held high, gave him a challenging look of my own. "Nope. No, I have not."

I slipped into the dark apartment in front of him.

CHAPTER THREE

CONOR

Maybe I was wrong about this chick.

She had a bit of a bite, and I liked it.

I reached over to hit the switch, bathing the living area of my apartment in bright light. Stepping away from the door, I stood back and waited for the door to latch before moving toward Curly.

"Grand tour," I said, giving my general spiel. I tossed the pad and invite down on the coffee table before gesturing in the direction of the couch. "Living room." I pointed to the kitchen, which was clear due to the lack of wall between the two spaces. "Kitchen slash dining." I stepped past Curly, skirting my comfortable, well-worn leather couch, and headed toward the sinlge hall in this place. Assuming she'd follow, I pointed to a door as we passed it. "Half bath." I kept walking to the end of the hall, heading toward the only other door, and walked into the bedroom.

This fucker was bigger than the living room and kitchen combined.

I had a California king in the middle of the far wall. A leather ottoman thing at the end of the bed. A dresser. A huge ass television. Door to the attached bathroom. Nothing horribly special in there yet, but I wanted to at least redo the shower. Nix the tub.

When Rory and I bought the bar from my parents, one of my projects was renovating the apartment above as well. Rory had his own place due to some investments he made in college, so I got to call the apartment my own. It had been a two bedroom with an office, and I wanted it to be a bitchin' bachelor pad.

Dream it, do it, you know?

"Bedroom. Where the magic happens," I finally said, turning to watch as Curly walked into the room behind me.

Usually the woman would say something at this point, or start stripping, something, but Curly just looked around. I followed her with my eyes as she stepped past me, moving along the wall and taking it in.

"It's a bit big for just you, don't you think?" she finally asked. She had stopped near the bed but turned toward me.

"The room or the bed? The bed is sometimes too small." I smirked at the memories.

Four women. One at the head, sitting with her legs spread. Another between her, eating her out. Me eating *that* one out while on my back and another woman bouncing on my cock, my hands buried in the fourth's wet, slick, bare pussy while she rubbed her tit and girl two's tit.

Good times had been had in this room.

Good times.

Curly looked like she was torn between shock and rolling her eyes. I liked the shock factor.

"Strip," I told her, reaching behind my head to pull off my shirt. No more talking shit. Down to business. I wanted her naked and spread on my bed.

I had an ache in my cock that having her fucking eyes on me caused. All damn night, she stared. Every fucking time she bit that damn lip of hers, I got a little harder.

It had been a long night downstairs, and I was long and thick to prove it.

When my shirt cleared my head, I saw that she had done the same, leaving her in just those fucking skinny jeans and a bra.

Her tits were fucking huge on her body. They weren't the perkiest I'd seen, nor the fullest, but tits were tits. Her belly and hips were soft, but she had a small gem hanging in her navel, showing me she wasn't one of those insecure girls who thought a little extra meat meant she was fat. The piercing proved it; she wasn't afraid to show off her belly.

I moved to sit on the bed, grinning to myself when she shifted at my nearness. I had a huge fucking bed and yes, I was going to sit next to her as I finished undressing.

I leaned forward to remove my boots and socks. I stood again so I could remove the kilt and my black boxers from underneath.

"You're moving slow, Curly."

I dropped everything and stepped out of the puddle of clothes, standing bare in front of this curly-haired woman.

I saw her rake her gaze over my body, lingering on my thick, hard cock that was pulsing and purple, straight the fuck up and down, needing a pussy to envelope it.

Her fingers faltered at the button of her jeans. That's right, Curly, I was fucking hung.

The women loved it. Often I was told it was my best asset.

And let's be honest. I wasn't looking for a relationship, so who the fuck cared if the best thing about me was my cock and what I could do with it?

"Get on with it, Curly Locks, or else your jeans won't make it home with you."

I liked nothing more than ripping clothes off a woman, and depending on the chick, I would do it without warning.

Curly lowered the zipper on her jeans antagonizingly slow, but when I caught her eyes, I saw just a hint of mischief there. Girl knew what she was doing.

She lowered them with a bit of a shimmy and when they were off, leaving her in her bra and, to my disappointment, plain cotton boy shorts, I grabbed her hips and pushed her back onto the bed. Her eyes flared wide for a moment but I dropped my mouth to the top of her tit, sucking and biting.

She let out a breathy moan when my mouth continued its way down until my I surrounded her covered nipple.

I sucked her into my mouth, my teeth gently biting down around the globe, and my tongue pressing against the pebbled peak there. I scraped my teeth back as I lifted my head, leaving a wet circle where my mouth had been.

Curly lay under me, her hips moving against the bed but she kept her hands off me. I needed more participation from her.

"Hands on my cock."

I pulled down the fabric cupping her breasts and groaned at the sight of her erect, puffy nipples. Damn, I loved puffies. The way they felt in my mouth, an extra cushion around a pebbled, hard peak.

Her hands finally grabbed me and in reward, I dove for her other nipple, sucking her deep into my mouth while my hands went to her underwear. If she were in a fucking thong, I'd rip the damn thing off her.

Or pull it to the side and sink into her.

But she was in fucking granny panties, and I had to actually remove the damn things.

I suckled on her tit while her hands slowly moved up and down my shaft. My girth was my truest asset, and I could feel she had her hands locked together, completely covering me with her hands, as she moved up and down.

I pulled back from her tit, allowing my teeth to bite down a bit harder than what could be considered gentle, and reveled in her open mouthed moan. Fuck yes, Curly.

Sitting back on my knees, I covered her breasts with my hands, kneading and pushing the globes together then apart. I fucking loved real tits. Her hands faltered on my cock but that was ok. I pushed back, my hands still on her chest, until I was partially leaning over her. I moved my hands from her tits only so I could finally undress her fully.

I pulled the offending cotton from her, leaving her bra on and under her tits, pushing them up, and groaned at the site of her bare pussy.

With her curly hair and normal attire, I would have pegged her for all natural. Maybe bikini-kept, but not fucking bare as a baby's bottom.

Still kneeling, but now between her legs, I took her ankles and folded her legs up and out so her wet, pink pussy was on display. My mouth watered as I saw her squeeze, a drop of her wetness seeping out of her. She was fucking soaked.

There would be no dry, uncomfortable penetration. She was going to be a slick, slippery glove and my cock weeped its own precum in anticipation.

Needing a taste of her, I leaned down and into her, sweeping my tongue over her beautiful folds. My hands were still on her ankles, but I could feel as her knees dropped inward toward my head. She moved her hips as if trying to get away from my mouth, but I wasn't having it.

One taste of her honey sweetness wasn't going to be enough.

I wasn't one for the foreplay, but her taste was fucking addicting.

I let go of one of her ankles so I could wrap my arm around her leg, laying my forearm over her hips to hold her down. As I put my mouth to her again, this time sucking and moving my face against her, I put my hand to the back of her other leg, pushing her thigh closer to her hip. The action trapped my hand against her but it also opened her up for me. Not wide with full access to her clit, but long, giving me access to her entire pussy and the puckered rose at her back.

Her hips bucked under my arm as I went to town on her. Sucking, thrusting, biting, nipping. My tongue flicked over her clit, then entered her pussy. I sucked and feasted on her wetness as she bucked and moaned and whispered my name. Her hands were in my hair, fisting the locks so fucking hard it hurt.

Give me more, Curly.

Pain with pleasure was the best line to cross.

I released my hold of her leg and her heel dropped to the bed beside me. I wasn't giving her an inch, though, as I sunk two fingers into her wet, waiting pussy.

Her breath came out as a sob and her hips jolted with the intrusion.

She was swollen against my fingers and so fucking tight, I wanted to weep at the thought of her surrounding my fucking cock. It was going to be a tight fit, if the feel of my fingers in her was any indication.

Because two fingers was nowhere close to my girth.

I pumped and pulsed my fingers into her quickly, so fucking fast my forearm was tight and I knew it would be slightly sore later in that night. But her squirming, her moans, her fucking squeezing so hard I thought my fingers would squeeze out of her, only egged me on to go harder and faster.

I sucked her clit into my mouth one last time before she shattered around me.

MIA

God damn, this was so much better than my toys.

The high I felt as I exploded around his hand was unlike any orgasm I ever gave myself.

I loved his control. His mouth was fucking magical and his fingers…

Damn.

Earlier, when he had me grab his cock, I was slightly fearful of his size. He was a bit bigger than my largest dildo.

I was always sexually minded, having started to masturbate at around twelve. I just never found time to date and never wanted to participate in meaningless sex.

Not that this with Conor wasn't meaningless.

He didn't even know who the hell I was. I think that gave the definition to meaningless.

The thought of sex always left me wet. Reading sex always left me uncomfortable with need. So finally last year, I decided to do something about it, and bought my first toy.

Which only spurred my desire for more.

When I started experimenting with penetrating toys, I started small, gradually getting to what was marketed as a normal sized penis.

Conor was not the same size. He was well-endowed in comparison.

I'd always questioned the thicker penises when watching porn, but now I knew they could be real and true.

He was thick from base to just before his head, where he

narrowed slightly before the rim of the head of his penis flared out. He was red with a slightly purple hue, with thick veins running up and down his length.

I knew that him entering me was going to be tight and probably a little uncomfortable, but I wasn't about to tell him I was a virgin.

I was on such a wonderful high, there was no fucking way I was allowing him to stop.

I lay there, my chest heaving as I came off of said high. His fingers were still buried deep inside of me but his mouth was no longer on me. Nor was his arm holding my hips down.

He was sitting back on his knees when he slowly, God, so fucking slowly, removed his fingers from my slick channel.

His curled fingers hit another nerve ending, causing me to squeeze down around him as I moaned. He chuckled and took his fingers from me. I watched in fascination as he put his fingers deep into his mouth, his bearded cheeks seeming to hollow as he sucked and pulled his fingers back out of his mouth.

Before I could tell him my thoughts on the action, his hand was fisting his cock and he grunted. "On your stomach."

I had a moment of panic. Maybe now was actually a really good time to—

Before I could further contemplate it, his hands were at my hips and he flipped me over, pulling me up on my knees so my ass was in the air. I rearranged my arms so my hands were at my shoulders, leaving my cheek pressed to the cream pillow that matched the dark tan spread under my body. Behind me, I heard the tear of foil just before I felt Conor's hands on my ass, pulling my cheeks apart.

I looked over my shoulder just as I felt the tip of his covered cock at my pussy.

Could he tell? Surely he wouldn't be able to tell I hadn't truly had sex, right? It would just be a little snug.

I risked looking up at his eyes, but his eyes were focused where his cock head rested. He removed one hand to position himself and I had to bite down on my lip at the excitement that this was happening.

I was nervous, sure, but I was more excited. Feeling the head of his cock right there...

And when he slammed into me, I had to turn my head into the pillow to muffle my yell.

God fucking damn, that hurt!

It was an unbearable stretch and I could feel tears prickling behind my eyes. I groaned open-mouthed into his pillow as his hands kneaded my love handles, his hips pushed all the way to my ass.

"God*damn*, you're so fucking tight, Curly." His voice was gritty and sexy, but I was too busy concentrating on relaxing my muscles. Deep breath in, letting it out slowly against the pillow.

I squeezed my eyes shut as he pulled out unhurriedly and thrust in again.

I could feel him sliding against my slickness, and the tightness was slowly becoming bearable. It was still slightly uncomfortable but he was moving in and out of me slowly, allowing me to become accustomed to his girth.

For the moment anyway.

His hands squeezed my hips as he continued his slow thrusting. "So wet, so tight."

Finally feeling composed, I turned my head so my cheek was to the pillow again. I tried to push up on my arms, but he moved a hand to between my shoulders and pressed me down.

"Right there. Stay right there for me, Curly."

He pushed himself to the brink again and I could feel as he shifted on his knees. Doing what, I wasn't sure. Moving closer?

With his cock still lodged deep in me, he moved my knees together as he straddled them. The new position with my legs together made the feel of him in me impossibly tighter, but I could feel every ridge and line of him as he began his slow pumping once again.

I needed more now, though.

The feel of him in me, thick and veiny and *full*, was bringing out something in me I had never felt before. I pushed my hips back to his, meeting his thrust with one of my own.

He chuckled above me. "Oh, you want more, do you? I'll give you more of this cock." His hands moved from my hips to just above my ass, pulling the extra there up and squeezing the handfuls. I ought to be embarrassed or self-conscious, but he didn't seem to mind as he squeezed and began pounding into me at a quicker pace.

"So fucking tight. Damn, Curly. Take me. Take all of me. That's right, woman. Take my cock."

His grunts intermixed with dirty words as his hips went from his quicker pace, to faster, shorter strokes, the head of his cock hitting me in all the right places. I thought for sure I was going to explode around him.

"I'm close," I managed to whisper.

"Tell me how much you want this cock. Tell me with your filthy mouth, woman. Don't you fucking come until you do."

My heart was pounding and I could feel nerve endings sizzle. How did one *stop* an impending orgasm? I didn't know, but I also didn't want him to stop doing what he was doing, so I did as he demanded.

"You're so big and full. I love when you hit—" I stopped on a moan as he did just as I was about to tell him.

"That? You like that. Tell me more. I'm gonna come so fucking hard, tell me."

I wasn't sure if he was informing me he was going to come, or if I was supposed to repeat him. Either way, it was likely true.

"I need to come, Conor. I have to come. I'm going to come so hard."

"Fucking hard."

"So fucking hard." I squeezed my eyes shut as my orgasm was right there, right at the brink. But I wasn't falling yet. I was right there and I needed to fall over the edge, I needed it so badly.

Conor wrapped an arm under my boobs and lifted me back to him, my back to his chest, as he continued to pound up into me. But it was his other hand that gave me the reprieve I was looking for.

His thick, calloused fingers were at my clit and he squeezed the nub between two fingers, just hard enough to send me flying.

I threw my head back against his shoulder as my mouth dropped open on a soundless cry. With all the porn I had watched, I just assumed a powerful orgasm would bring out the vocals, but I stayed whisper silent, like I did when getting myself off.

"Goddamn, Curly. Fuck!" His cock pushed up into me and I could feel him throbbing against my own pulsing and tightening. It was a heady feeling, the battling beats warring inside my pussy.

Before I was fully sated, Conor lowered us more gently than I would have guessed he was capable of until my stomach was back to the mattress. My legs straightened and before I could revel in the feel of his weight on my back, Conor pulled out of me and stood from his bed.

"Damn. I may just keep you around for a repeat after my cock is rested." He chuckled to himself and I rolled to my back in time to see him frown, moving his hands to roll the condom off his softening dick. "The condom broke. Probably because you were so fucking tight. You're on the pill, right?" He didn't sound anxious. "I'm clean. Get tested regularly. You clean, Curly?" He moved to the bathroom, leaving me alone in his room, in the middle of his huge bed.

Those were not words a girl wanted to hear when she *wasn't* on the pill. Especially when said so nonchalantly.

My doctor put me on a number of birth control pills in my teens to help with hormone regulation due to my period being incredibly irregular, but they all made me severely depressed. I stopped trying to find one that worked. By twenty-two, my hormones finally settled but my period stayed regularly irregular.

"Um." I could tell him no, I wasn't. I'm sure this wasn't his first rodeo with a broken condom, not with how easily he announced it. Or I could just tell him yes and be sure to go to the doctor right away in the morning.

If I had had time to plan this night with Conor, I would have made an appointment with my doctor prior to the planned night, but that hadn't been in the cards.

I sat up then, pulling the cups of my bra up over my breasts and looking around for the rest of my clothing.

I heard a toilet flush and Conor walked back into the room. "You didn't answer me, Curly."

"Um, yeah. I am." I shook my head and forced a grin on my face, looking around until I spotted my underwear. Good God, I wore *those* today?

My face slightly red, I stood and reached for them. I pulled the plain cotton on as Conor grabbed a clean pair of boxers from one of his dressers. He turned toward me as he stepped into the fabric and I risked looking at his penis, curious what it looked like flaccid.

He wasn't nearly as long, but he was still pretty thick. It was impressive, really.

I grabbed my shirt and slipped it on over my head before finding my jeans. This whole getting dressed immediately after sex was awkward. It wasn't something I wanted to do again.

Conor came over to the bed as I was hopping into my jeans and I noticed another frown marring his face.

"What the fuck?" It came out as a surprised whisper, his brows drawn in as he stared at the bed.

I looked behind me and bit my lip.

So much for that theory.

CHAPTER FOUR

CONOR

It had been a fun, even if slightly quick, session in the sack, and I was ready to hit that sack for other reasons. It was nearing three thirty and I'd been up since five the morning prior. Curly was getting dressed and when she'd been putting on her shirt, I admired her soft stomach and full tits once more before she bent to pull on her jeans.

Which gave me a better view of those tits.

It was over her shoulder, though, that I noticed the small dark marks on the spread.

I walked closer and took a better look, my eyes frowning.

"What the fuck?"

She'd been too wet to tear, even with how fast I pushed myself to the hilt.

Which only meant...

No.

She was tight, but I had only heard stories of girls being so tight, with breaking through the hymen, that it was nearly chokingly tight around the guy's dick.

My frown still in place, I looked down at Curly. She was now standing at her full height, her hands clasped in front of her and her eyes...

Shit, her eyes looked worried.

"Were you a fucking virgin?"

She bit that lip of hers again and my damn cock warred with my head.

"I said, were you a fucking virgin?"

I didn't fuck virgins. I didn't.

Fuck. She was going to want to come back, she was going to cling. I didn't do relationships, and I certainly didn't do second-times, unless the second time was with a group.

Curly lifted her chin defiantly. "I'll see myself out. Thanks for a great time, Conor."

I reached for her arm to pull her to a stop. I was angry, yes, but when she flinched at the movement, I had a moment of realization that between my anger, my words, my actions, and then I'm sure with the way I looked…

"Get your hand off of me," she said between clenched teeth.

I let go of her arm and held both my hands up. I tried for a more placid tone, but even I could hear it didn't quite make it. "Were you. A virgin."

I could see her battling the answer. I could see her battling answering me.

Fuck.

Her chin still lifted, her brown eyes met mine and held. There was a long moment of silence before she opened her mouth again. "Yes."

Fuck.

I didn't want to be insensitive but… I was. I was insensitive.

"Why didn't you say anything?"

"I didn't think you would notice." She moved to walk out of the room and I followed. Willingly, even.

"How the fuck wouldn't I notice?"

She didn't bother to stop or turn her head to look at me. "You didn't until well after the fact."

Lady had a point.

"Look." She finally stopped in the living room, turning toward me. "I was curious and I'd heard about you and I just wanted the damn thing taken care of. That's all. I'm not going to cling. I'm not going to beg you for tomorrow night. In fact, you probably won't ever see me again." She smiled slightly, but it looked menacing almost. "Thank you for tonight, Conor," she said again. "I'll see myself out."

She turned again and moved to the other side of the room

in record time. I tried telling myself I didn't care, she was just another chick, another hole on another night.

But when she reached the door and looked over her shoulder at me briefly before pulling the door open and stepping out, I was hit in the gut again with her familiarity.

But I didn't know her.

Shit, she was just another woman I took to bed who I didn't get her name. Names didn't matter.

But for whatever reason, I had a feeling her name mattered. A feeling that her being my first, and fuck she'd better be my only, virgin, mattered.

I shook my head.

I was too tired for this shit.

Tomorrow night I'd take two girls. That would take my mind off Curly for sure.

CHAPTER FIVE

LATE AUGUST

CONOR

"Get your fucking phone out of the ice chest, Rory."

Rory and I were getting the bar ready for the day. It was all of ten on a Sunday morning but with a noon baseball game, we were bound to start getting busy the moment we opened the doors at eleven.

"Dude, yesterday there was a Articuno in here."

I frowned at my kid brother. "A what?"

"Articuno. You know, Pokémon Go?" Rory closed the ice chest and scanned his phone around the bar and into one of the fridges.

"You are fucking twenty-nine years old, Rory. Pokémon is for ten year olds."

Rory shook his head, his longer wavy hair shaking with the movement. "No. Definitely more adults playing. It's like a flashback from childhood." Still, Rory didn't look away from his phone.

I walked over to him and snatched the device from him. "Well right now we need to get the bar ready, so catch your Pikachu on your own fucking time."

Rory grabbed for his phone but I did the dick move and put it down the front of my pants.

"Fuck, Con! Shit, that's nasty." Rory's face was contorted and I couldn't help but laugh as I went back to my earlier task. "You owe me a new phone, fucker."

"I didn't put it down my boxers. Relax, man." I shook my

head, grinning. I was stacking glasses when Brenna came barreling into the bar from the swinging kitchen door.

"Oh my God, you'll never guess who I ran into last night!"

I looked over my shoulder at my twenty-five year old baby sister. Her black hair matched my own, but had the same waves Rory's did, although hers was much longer.

"Oh, please do tell," I said dryly. Whether Rory or I wanted to hear, Brenna would tell. She probably ran into one of her ex's that was a douche, that Rory or I took care of. Something or someone like that.

"Mia Hampton."

I moved to grab another pallet of glasses and glanced at Brenna. "Mia Hampton?" Remembering the phone in my pants, I took it out and put it in my back pocket. Brenna caught the act and frowned a moment before continuing her story.

"You know. Curly Mia from elementary school? My best friend up until the fifth grade? She spent every freaking day at our house."

Rory chuckled. "Oh yeah. Fat Mia."

"Rory!" Brenna's brows were raised. "She wasn't *fat*. Don't be a dick."

"She was kind of pudgy," I said under my breath.

"You two are asses." Brenna crossed her arms. "Anyway, I saw her at the mall. Get this. Coming out of a *maternity* store. She's gotta be like...six months pregnant. I asked about her husband and she doesn't have one. Said the baby was an accident but she looked so happy. *God*! Remember how everyone thought I was the bad egg between the two of us? Shit. Who'd have thought she'd get knocked up on accident...before I did." Brenna stumbled on the last of her words and while that was concerning, I didn't question it.

"Great?" I didn't really care who was pregnant or that pudgy Mia from fifteen years ago was without a man and with a child. I wasn't about to call Brenna out on spreading stories though. She knew what harm could come from them and I didn't really want to see her bright eyes dim at the reminder.

"Anyway, I invited her out to dinner tonight."

I paused and looked at her. "Tonight's your birthday dinner."

She nodded, grinning.

I scratched above my eyebrow, slightly exasperated with her. "Why would you invite her to a dinner you were having with your brothers? Go do lunch with her instead. It's not like you work here."

"I do too work here, asshole." Brenna uncrossed her arms. "She just looked kind of lonely. Happy, yeah, but lonely, and I thought it would be nice for her to meet up with everyone again."

I shook my head. My sister was so softhearted sometimes.

Rory shrugged a shoulder as he faced the liquors on the back shelf. "So we do dinner with pudgy Mia—"

"Don't call her that!"

Rory continued, ignoring Brenna. "It's just one night, Con. Make nice, you asshole."

I couldn't help but feel like Brenna was setting one of us up with Mia. Rory, the Pokémon Go player, certainly wasn't up to dating a woman who was knocked up, and me? Fuck that shit.

"She's actually really pretty," Brenna added, her brows up and a sly grin on her face. And that fucking look was aimed at me.

Yep, totally trying to set me up.

I pointed at her. "Do not."

She feigned innocence and lifted her hands in the air. "I'm not doing anything, Con!"

"I like my life."

"I know!" She put her hands down. "I just thought maybe if you saw her again, you would maybe think twice about all the hoes in your life." She grinned at me. "Besides, I miss having her in my life. She was a good friend."

"You were fucking ten."

"Hey! That's a pretty impressionable time in a young girl's life!"

"She ditched you."

"Yep, she totally did," Rory added, as if he were actually a part of this tennis match and not an onlooker. Speaking of, the fucker wasn't working.

"Rory. Do something with the bar." Then to Brenna, "I don't do relationships, Bren. You know that. I'll make nice at dinner, but don't expect anything more."

The answering look on Brenna's face...

I didn't want to know what she had up her sleeve.

And quite frankly, at the moment I didn't care. I had a bar to run.

MIA

Living in the town I grew up in had its moments.

Moments where I wished I'd chosen a teaching job anywhere else.

Unfortunately, of the schools I was offered a job at, the neighboring town of Imperial Beach, where I spent much of my youth, had the better program. As such, I taught second grade at an elementary school I went to, and often ran into old classmates at the grocery store.

Or ex-best friends at the mall. Namely, an ex-best friend whose brother put this big old basketball in this tummy of mine.

You know. People like that.

When Brenna asked about my husband, I froze. When she rephrased to ask about the "baby daddy," I stumbled and looked at my feet. I wasn't about to tell her my baby's daddy was her older brother. I hadn't even had the nerve to walk into the bar to tell him; I sure wasn't going to tell his sister first.

But somehow I found myself doing just that, as I cried over an iced tea in the food court. I didn't know why Brenna was being so nice to me, but she was extremely easy to talk to and there I was, blubbering at her like a freaking fool.

"Conor? My Conor?" she had asked.

I nodded and told her how he didn't know who I was, and how it was just a one-night thing. How I never intended on seeing him again but after my irregular period was nearing three months late, I took the test and my stomach had dropped. What were the freaking odds I'd get pregnant my first time, and for

Plan B failing too? It was as if the Gods were laughing at me, making an example out of the good girl who did one naughty thing.

Brenna simply hugged me and went on and on about how she and I could finally be close again. About how she was going to help me break the news to her brother. About how she and I could discuss it over dinner tomorrow night.

I was extremely thrown by this bombardment from Brenna but needing a friend, I took her up on her offer.

I had gone home and tried to find an outfit that didn't make me feel like a whale. Now wearing it, I found myself at a cute Italian restaurant just outside of town.

I sat by the front door, nervously chewing on my lip as I waited for Brenna to show. She told me to meet her just outside the door and text her the moment I arrived.

I held my clutch in front of me, nervous energy running through me. I was still a bit put off by the whole running into Brenna and her wanting to be my friend after fifteen years thing, but I would get past it.

The doors swung open and out walked Brenna in her raven-haired glory. It really was unfair that she'd been beautiful as a pre-teen and was even more gorgeous as an adult. What happened to that adage of the pretty ones turning out to be the ugliest after school was over?

"Come on in. I have a table already." Brenna smiled and held the door for me, allowing me to step into the restaurant before she moved in front to weave the way to the table.

I should have followed my gut when I felt the telltale signs of something being wrong the moment I left the mall—and Brenna—yesterday.

Because just a few tables away, a few feet in front of Brenna, was Conor.

I stopped dead in my tracks and, whether it was hormones or just me, felt tears build up behind my eyes. I was so fucking naïve.

Of course, she didn't want to be my friend. She stopped

wanting to be my friend in middle school when I was too fat to hang out with her. When she was getting all the attention from boys and I was in the middle of my extremely long awkward phase.

Was her inviting me tonight her being facetious? Was she being rude and wanting to point fingers at me? What the hell was her goal?

The buzzing in my head didn't allow for me to hear Brenna address the table but the moment Conor's eyes met mine across the short distance, my stomach truly dropped to the floor, my clutch following shortly after.

With a red face and burning eyes, I knelt down the best I could with my slightly protruding belly, and picked up my clutch. I stood as gracefully as I could in the black pants and flowy shirt that did *not* hide the evidence underneath and, with a swallow, made myself face Conor.

Made myself face the father of my child.

CHAPTER SIX

CONOR

The after-game crowd had been a bit of a riot at O'Gallaghers, but Rory and I managed to slip out in time to make it to dinner with Brenna. Stone was manning the bar for me, and I had full trust in the man.

Never mind the fact it was Sunday, and we would only be open for another hour or so.

As soon as we made it to our table for our seven o'clock reservations, Brenna excused herself to go meet Mia.

I should have figured there was more to Brenna's excitement than her simply running into an old friend who was pregnant.

Because when Brenna came back, big-ass grin on her face, with Mia behind her...

My stomach fucking dropped.

Mia was Curly Locks.

Curly Locks was Mia.

The chick I fucked, the only virgin I fucked, nearly half a fucking year ago, was pregnant.

I would like to think that my sexual prowess persuaded Curly, *Mia*, to go get laid more often, that there was no fucking way in hell that that baby bump had anything to do with me, but I wasn't stupid.

Fuck.

Fuck.

I hardcore stared at her. She looked the same as all those nights ago, except for the obvious being pregnant. That and her curly mass of hair was down, a small top section pulled back with everything else falling just past her shoulders.

I was so fucking torn. Mia was goddamn hot and I can't say I ever found a pregnant woman sexy before. But putting my cock aside, she had known who the hell I was and still fucked me.

How the *hell* didn't she tell me who she was? So not only did I fuck a virgin, but I fucked a girl who used to follow me around like a sick puppy dog, up until she and my sister had a falling out.

The real kicker though, the one that got me in the balls, was just like she hadn't found it important to tell me her name, she hadn't found it important to tell me I knocked her up.

Mia's eyes met mine across the tables and I watched as her face went from bright red to fucking pale as a ghost, no doubt in response to the fire in my eyes. *That's right, bitch. I'm pissed.*

"Brenna," I growled low. I wasn't about to make a scene in this fancy-assed restaurant, but I needed a word with my sister. Brenna's grin faltered and the light went out from her eyes. I had a fleeting thought that maybe she wasn't being cruel in this meeting.

But then again, this was the girl who left my baby sister to fend for herself when the adolescent years started to get tough.

She shot a small smile over her shoulder at Mia before walking over to where I still sat at the table. Her brows pulled low, the growl in her whispered voice matched my earlier one as she leaned down, her face in mine. "You will fucking make nice, Conor O'Gallagher."

"I love you, and it's your birthday, but I am not dealing with *that*," I pointedly glared toward Mia, who was still clutching her wallet in front of her, "at your dinner. I trust you have her phone number, so send her away and I'll deal with her later."

I couldn't believe that Curly Locks was Mia. No shit her eyes had looked familiar. I'd seen them nearly every day from when she and Brenna were three until they were ten.

"I'm not sending her away!" Brenna whisper yelled at me.

"What the fuck game are you playing?" I glanced over when I noticed Rory stand and watched as he walked over to Mia, no doubt to make small talk for both her and his own sanity.

Probably was bored being out of the loop.

It didn't explain the tightening in my chest or the red in my eye when Mia smiled at Rory and hugged him. What the fuck was that about?

"I'm not playing a game. You did this, Conor, you did." Brenna poked her finger into my chest. "*You* will make nice and *you* will make this right."

"She didn't even fucking tell me her name."

Brenna lifted a brow, standing straight and crossing her arms over her chest. "How many names do you usually take when you bring one of your 'hoes upstairs, Conor? She was just another and you knocked her up."

Again, that fucking tightening in my chest when Brenna essentially called Mia my whore.

What the actual fuck? I rubbed my chest, but did it where Brenna had jabbed her finger into my sternum.

"Why are you being nice to her, Bren?" I looked around quickly.

Surely we were making a scene with two of us arguing over hushed words, and two others awkwardly having a conversation. "She abandoned you. At fucking ten years old, Brenna! She should mean nothing to you."

Brenna's face morphed into one of almost sadness as she shrugged, her brows lifted. "Maybe I was the one to abandon her. And I don't want to do it again. We may not have been friends, but I always knew she wasn't one to spread the rumors."

"It's your dinner. Whatever." I shook my head, knowing I wasn't going to win this. My fault or not, Mia had known who I was. She also had known where to fucking find me and chose not to.

I shook my head, turning my attention back to the empty table, and tossed my napkin in my lap roughly. Brenna sat beside me and once she and I were seated, Rory and Mia walked over. Rory, showing off his fucking cocky side, held out the chair for Mia and she sat slowly across the table from me, her eyes glued to the table cloth.

I kept my eyes on Mia. I had so many things to say, cruel words, fucked up words, but also questions. Curious questions. Rory sat down beside her and reached for the wine menu.

"This calls for something strong." Rory flipped open the small booklet and started to scan, as if the kid knew a damn thing about a good wine.

Still, my eyes were on Mia. She kept her hands in her lap, gripping her clutch still, I assumed, her eyes remaining on the table. I watched as she started to lift them, stopping where the table met my stomach, and her eyes cut over toward Brenna.

Mia shook her head and swallowed roughly. "I can't do this." Her voice was strangled.

Brenna reached across the table, holding her palm up. "Mia. You two need to talk. I know my brother, and this is going to be the least hostile place for you two."

"Yeah. Besides, it's totally Con's fault you're in this predicament anyway so let him deal with the stares," Rory offered.

I frowned at him. "Thanks."

Rory grinned and winked. "No prob, bro."

Mia glanced at Brenna's hand finally and she started to lift her own from her clutch. Quickly though, I watched as her face went from slightly red in embarrassment to blanched, to a really fucking concerning shade of green. Rather than reach for Brenna's hand, Mia brought the back of her hand up to her mouth and with wide eyes, shook her head. "I'm going to be sick."

She stood from the table quickly and I could hear as her clutch fell to the floor again. She looked around the area quickly, looking for the bathroom, I would assume, and left the table in a hurry. I sat in my chair but turned to watch over my shoulder. I saw as she stumbled when someone pushed their chair out to stand, but she recovered and continued her trek.

Brenna took my shoulder and forced me to turn back to the table.

"She's twenty-four weeks pregnant and she's under the illusion that it's yours. And after the story she told me, I have to say I believe her," Brenna said, her voice in that low, dangerous tone again. She was pissed at me.

"She didn't tell me who she was," I repeated.

"That doesn't fucking matter, Con! She's pregnant and she's alone, and she's obviously scared of you! Did you see the way she looked at you? What the hell did you do? Tie her up against her will? Slap her around?"

Rory, the bastard, looked ready to laugh as he settled into his chair, arms crossed over his chest.

"I may have raised my voice when I learned she was a virgin."

"A...?" Brenna frowned. "She was a twenty-five-year-old virgin? No way. She's too pretty and too confident."

"She was a fucking virgin." I squeezed the bridge of my nose between my finger and thumb.

Rory still looked smug, but he turned his chin some and an inquisitive look crossed his face. "You ever get anyone pregnant before, Con? I mean, you do have quite the active sex life." As if he had room to fucking talk.

Brenna put her fingers to her ears. "Lalala, I don't wanna hear it!"

I frowned at Brenna but then turned back to Rory. "Not that I know of, no." I pulled Brenna's finger from her ear and said loudly enough in her direction, but not so loud the entire restaurant would hear. "The condom broke when I was in her tight pussy."

"You're such a pig," Brenna muttered before I turned back to Rory.

"I've only broken a condom maybe two other times and I've seen those chicks getting plastered afterward, so I'm going to go with no."

"Well, congrats, Daddy," Rory said with a shit-eating grin. Bastard.

Brenna looked over her shoulder to where Mia disappeared to. "I'm going to go check on her."

I stood before Brenna could. "I'll do it."

She and I needed to have words.

In private.

CHAPTER SEVEN

MIA

Thank God I made it to the bathroom in time. I didn't bother locking the door to the single person bathroom, only caring to dive for the toilet before what was sure to be only stomach acid came up and out of my mouth.

I was too late in the game to be having morning sickness and actually, I had been extremely lucky my first trimester, never getting sick. I never had cravings, I didn't have the need to binge eat. The only change in my life was the fact I was growing another life inside of me.

Having not eaten since noon, the only thing that came up was indeed stomach acid. The burning in my throat, paired with the embarrassment of the entire situation I found myself in tonight, had tears falling from my eyes.

I was such a fucking fool for believing that Brenna would want to renew a friendship. Who sought out a friendship from someone you hadn't truly spoken to since middle school?

I should have figured she was going to throw Conor in my face. I never told her when we were little, but I think she always knew I had crushed on her oldest brother.

But what was a crush at ten? It was a whole lot of *nothing*.

I wiped the back of my mouth and reached for the toilet paper, needing to blot some of the wetness from my cheeks when there was a knock at the door.

"Just a minute!" I called out, a slight wavering in my voice that was no doubt due to the tears in my eyes.

I stood and straightened out my dress pants, trying to dust off the knees. When the baby moved, I put my hand over the front of my swelling tummy. "It's ok, baby."

I chose not to find out if I was having a boy or a girl. I still had moments where I considered putting the baby up for adoption. Was I ready to be a mom? Was I ready to be a single parent?

I wanted this baby, but sometimes it was the fear of what I could offer the child, or rather what I *couldn't* offer him or her, that kept me up at night.

The knock on the door sounded yet again. Damn impatient woman. I glanced at the mirror after moving to the sink and grimaced at the splotches on my face. "Just a second, I'm sorry."

I turned on the water and just began splashing water on my face when the door swung open.

I jerked up and turned to face the intruder. "I said it would just be a min—"

Conor.

My heart stopped and yet again, I could feel the color fall from my face.

He stepped into the small space and closed the door behind him, doing what I failed to do and locking the door.

Locking the two of us in here together.

I swallowed hard and stared at him. He stared back.

I took in his dress pants and dress shirt, sleeves rolled up to show off the gray and black sleeve he had on his left arm. His beard appeared to be freshly kept and his eyes, framed with such dark, thick lashes, were locked on mine.

It wasn't fair he was such a beautiful man.

"Why didn't you tell me?" Conor broke the silence with a surprisingly calm voice.

Tell him what? My name? That I was pregnant?

"Because I was afraid of your response," I finally answered. It was the truth and fit both scenarios. I forced my eyes to meet his, and altered my gaze from his left to his right eye, back and forth as I tried to read his expression.

He hadn't been happy to see me out there.

But then again, I hadn't been exactly thrilled, either.

Just like I'd been attempting a plan to get into Conor's bed, I had been trying to figure out a way to tell him, oops, that broken condom left me a little pregnant.

"You keeping it?" His eyes jerked down to my tummy then back up to mine.

"It's a little too late to abort," I said a little harsher than the situation probably warranted for. Besides, medically that was a lie.

He shook his head and sighed. I could feel his annoyance with me. "I meant adoption. Are you giving it up?"

I put my hands on my belly as if trying to protect the little one tucked away inside. I gave Conor the truth. "I've considered the fact that I might not be what's best for this baby, but I think," I took a deep breath. Everything clicked into place. Regardless of Conor and what happened in the future, yes, I wanted this baby. "Yeah," I nodded. "I'm keeping it."

His blue gaze was once again locked on my stomach, this time not moving. "You want child support or something? After a DNA test, of course." His eyes met mine again and I fought the need to yell at him. Rather, I clenched my jaw.

"If I wanted something from you, Conor, I would have sought you out."

"Oh, like you did for your virginity. Because that's what that was about, right?" He crossed his arms over his chest. "You knew who the fuck I was, and still you sat at my fucking bar, eye fucking me every damn time you were there. You planned on me taking your virginity."

I lifted my chin and said through gritted teeth. "I didn't think you would notice. Because guess what?" When I was pissed, my mouth ran. And it was about to run. "Your cock's not the only thing that's been in this pussy. Get over yourself, fucker."

There was a red haze around the room and I had to fight the mixed urge to vomit and to run. My heart was pounding in both anxiety and anger. I tugged on the lower hem of my shirt which ended up only allowing the bulge of my tummy to show off even more, and pushed away to try and get past Conor, needing to leave.

Damn Conor for being a gorgeous asshole.

Damn Brenna for being a conniving bitch.

Fuck me for being naïve and believing the best in people.

Conor was standing in front of the door but I attempted to squeeze around him anyway. "Let me out." I leaned against him in an effort to push him out of the way, but I knew I was going to fail this battle.

With ease, Conor put his big hands on my arms and moved me away from the door and against a nearby wall.

"I told you once before. Keep your Goddamn hands off of me." Again, I spoke through clenched teeth. It was that or I was afraid I was going to start crying. Damn fucking hormones.

"I seem to remember you liking my hands on you."

"Yeah, before your asshole colors truly came out." I refused to look him in the eye, instead choosing to look at his shoulder.

"You knew beforehand that I was an asshole. Everyone knows I'm an ass."

I worked on calming my heart before meeting his eyes with my own. "Please just let me go. I won't bother you with the baby. I promise." My voice cracked on the last word and I could feel the damn tears I tried so hard to keep at bay, fill my eyes.

This time it was Conor's eyes flitting back and forth between my own. His hands squeezed on my arms and once they loosened, I thought I would be able to run to freedom, never seeing him again.

But I was wrong.

Oh so wrong.

CONOR

Now that I knew she was Mia from back in the day, now that I had that small amount of knowledge, the familiarity in her eyes made so much sense. I looked back and forth between her whiskey brown eyes and when I saw them watering, it hit me low in the gut.

I wasn't a guy who dealt with emotion. My sister's, sure, yeah. But never anyone outside of my siblings.

I flirted with women at the bar because they tipped extremely well when I did. I took countless nameless women up to my apartment at the end of the night and they always knew the score. Bring them up, get *it* up, in, out, go home. Every night it was the same story and rarely did any of the women linger in my mind.

I thought that Curly lingering in my mind was because she'd been a virgin. It made her, unfortunately, special. And not necessarily special in a good way.

Special in a way that had me seeing red for weeks afterward.

But eventually I worked her out of my system by doing what I always did. But the shock of seeing her again, being pregnant no less, had all the feelings I thought I pushed down and away, coming back up.

Feelings that maybe she was special in a different way.

I didn't want a special woman in my life. I liked my life the way it was, thank you. I liked different pussy and multiple pussy. I liked rough sex, and bondage sex, and anal sex. Looking at this curly haired woman in front of me, I didn't see that in her.

But damn if that didn't have me turning away from her.

Rather, I did what I never did with women.

I loosened my grip from her arms, and just as I saw the relief flash through her eyes, I grabbed her hips and pulled her in tight. The swell of her stomach against my now hard, aching cock gave me pause, but not nearly as much as the need to kiss her did.

I didn't kiss women.

I didn't kiss men either, you fuckers.

I just didn't kiss. I put my mouth on pussies, dipped my tongue in them too, but my mouth never touched another's. Not really sure why, to be honest; kissing just never was high on my agenda. I always had other places I wanted my lips and tongue to be.

But at this moment, the only place I wanted them was on Mia's full, pink ones.

Her mouth opened on a gasp and I took the opportunity to

sweep my tongue inside. My hands gripped at her hips, and I fought the desperate need to pull her closer than she already was. Any closer and I'd be inside her, fucking her against the wall.

Not that that was a bad idea.

I reached around her to grab a handful of her delectable ass. She went up on tiptoe and finally, *finally* she was participating. Her hands were in my hair, her tongue battling mine. Mia tried pressing closer and she groaned in disappointment when she couldn't. I couldn't help but pull back just enough to chuckle.

"What do you need, Mia," I whispered against her mouth right before I nipped at her upper lip.

"You," she whispered back as she moved her hands out of my hair, her fingers grazing through my beard. She traced her fingers down my neck, my chest, my sternum. Down, down, she kept going down.

I kept my body still, not wanting to rush her pursuit but my cock was fucking ecstatic at the trail her hands were taking. Her fingers lingered at the top of my pants, just above my belt, where my shirt was tucked.

Untuck it, I wordlessly pleaded with her. *Untuck it and stick your hands down my pants, Mia. Do it.*

She kept a hand at the top of my belt buckle and with her palm, trailed over and down to where my cock was standing up and at attention, as best as it could against my pants. Her palm covered me and I bit back a moan. Fucking God, I needed her hand to squeeze me.

But be careful what you wish for, because—

"*Fucking A!*"

She fucking squeezed all right. She fucking squeezed so fucking hard, my hands fell from her and she stepped back.

Her face was flushed but her eyes still held that sheen of tears from before, and *that*, ladies and gentlemen, is what gave me the truest pause. She'd been into the kiss. I knew that she had been; she was more fucking responsive now than she had been in March.

"I said keep your hands off of me, Conor," she said, her lip quivering just slightly but her eyes held fire. She pulled down on her shirt—more in a nervous habit, if I had to guess, than to straighten it—and pushed her chin up. "Not everything can be answered with sex. When you're ready to be an adult and talk to me, I'll be happy to do just that."

This time when she pushed past me, I let her go, watching as she left the small confines of the bathroom.

I should be pissed. Fuck, my dick ached for a whole different reason at this very moment.

But rather than be pissed, I was slightly amused.

Mia had claws.

I couldn't wait to tame them.

CHAPTER EIGHT

MIA

I stomped out of the restroom, berating myself the entire way to the table where Brenna and Rory still sat.

I *enjoyed* his mouth on me. It was an action I wasn't expecting, and the way he controlled the kiss... My God, the man was magical.

And I *responded*. I was supposed to be pissed at him! I *was* pissed at him!

Sure, this whole debacle was my fault but my goodness, I didn't expect a *kiss* from him upon finding out that I was pregnant and had kept it from him!

I furiously swiped under my eyes, trying to rid my lower lids of any lingering tears. Fuck this hormonal emotional bull, too. I hated that I cried on a drop of a dime and from the moment Conor turned his icy glare at me, to when he was trying to win me over by getting in my pants yet again...

I couldn't control the emotions.

Brenna noticed me coming first and immediately stood. "I am so sorry, Mia."

I held up a hand as I drew near the table. "Save it, Brenna. I should have realized you had something up your sleeve. I wasn't good enough for you growing up, and you obviously wanted to push all my buttons now." Mia's mouth dropped open and she gaped at me. I was so livid, so *pissed*, with myself that I really could give two shits about Mia's thoughts and reactions at this very moment.

I looked around the table for my clutch, finally spotting it where my chair was. I leaned forward but grumbled to myself when my belly got in the way. My goodness, I didn't know what I would do in even five more weeks. At twenty-four weeks, I looked like I was harboring a ball of some sort under my shirt, and I still had sixteen weeks to go.

I moved my lean into a crouch and finally was able to retrieve my clutch. I stood back up just as Conor reached the table.

"Happy birthday, Bren," he said, pulling her in to kiss her temple, "but I'm taking Mia home."

"Like hell you are!" I slammed my clutch to my side.

He glared at me, the blue of his eyes icy and fierce. "I'm taking you home. We are not finished." Each word was pronounced as if he were forcing each word out. As if his forced words would get me to comply.

Ha!

I wasn't some woman he could just...order around! I shook my head. "No. I drove myself. I'll get myself home." I turned on my heel before he could get in another word.

With my head lowered, I made my way out of the restaurant. We definitely made quite the scene and it was embarrassing to say the least. Before I could open the door, it opened from a masculine arm behind me and I fought the need to growl at Conor.

I walked through the door, my clutch held firmly against my leg, as I made my way toward my car.

"I said I was taking you home," Conor spoke from behind me. He was right on my heels, not that I turned to check.

"And I said I was doing it myself." I weaved through the cars in the parking lot, finding my gray Mazda-3. I popped open my clutch to find the little fob I tossed in there, hitting the button to unlock the doors.

As I went to open the door though, Conor's big paw slapped down, holding the door in place.

"I want. To talk. To you."

I whipped around, my back to my car, before I could decide that was a bad move. I was now trapped between a menacing

Conor and his hard, delicious body, and my car, with no escape route.

"Then talk." I gave him my best stern-teacher voice, even though inside I was quivering with nerves. Or anticipation. I wasn't entirely sure which.

"Not out here."

I crossed my arms and drew in my brows. "You are *awfully* demanding."

"We need to talk, Mia, and I don't want to do it out in the open. My place, your place, *fuck,* the bar. Just not here."

He didn't move any closer, but he was already close enough. The toes of his boots met the toes of my shoes and with him leaning forward against the car, it brought his chest and neck close to my face. When I'd last been near him, he smelled good, yes, but he had the scent of the bar on him.

And other women.

Let's not forget the other women.

But tonight he was devoid the other smells. He was all Conor. All amber musk goodness.

I had to work to keep my mad on. It would be all too easy to fall into the charm of Conor O'Gallagher. When he flashed smiles or winks, when he was actually nice, he was incredibly attractive.

Come to think of it, I hadn't really experienced that side of Conor. I just watched it from the sidelines at the bar.

"Fine." I turned back toward my car. "But I'm driving myself. To my place. You can follow." I didn't want to be in his apartment. While it held a few moments of great memories for me, I didn't want to have a conversation with him in a place that he likely had forty other women in after I left.

I wasn't anything special. It wasn't like he went celibate after I went upstairs with him.

Conor dropped his arm from the car and stepped back. I ached for him to brush his hand along my arm, my lower back, *anywhere*, but he didn't. He kept his hands to himself. "All right. I'll follow."

CONOR

I followed behind Mia at her request. The entire drive to her place though had my mind swirling.

Where did she live? Was it safe for an infant? Did I really care if it was safe for a baby? Was I getting *invested* in this baby? If I was, what did that do for me and Mia?

Was there a me and Mia? Fuck, did I *want* a me and Mia?

Hell, I didn't even *know* Mia!

All these thoughts were confusing as shit. I liked my life. I liked the different women every night and the thought of settling down, the fucking *idea*, was never one that played in my head.

But one look at Curly walking back into my life, with a baby belly at that, had everything shifting, even if just slightly.

Mia pulled into a small, seemingly well-kept, apartment complex and I maneuvered my Subie into an open spot near her car port.

I was probably getting too old for the turbo charged, boosted Subaru, but it had been my dream car as a teenager, and I was holding on to her as long as her motor kept running.

So to all those fuckers who said I couldn't handle commitment, fuck you. I could handle commitment just fine.

I cut the ignition and peeled myself out of my car, not bothering to look across the lot before stalking toward Mia, who stood beside her own car waiting.

Thank fucking God, her eyes didn't have tears in them anymore. They still held that sass I witnessed in the restroom, but sass I could handle.

Before I could think up something to say, Mia turned and headed toward the building. I, having called this meeting, followed behind. I left enough room between us so I could check out the sway of her hips. One of the things I immediately noticed on Mia, beside her belly, was that her tits grew. I wasn't surprised then, to find her ass had a little extra bounce to it, too.

I wanted to put my hands on it, squeeze the round globes in my hands as I pounded into her from behind...

Wait a fucking second.

I didn't do double dipping. I know I said we needed to talk, and I know I was having some mixed feelings on the drive over, but hell if my head didn't seem to want to keep Mia around. I was going to have to think about that little fact a bit longer.

Mia had me climb three fucking flights of steps. Three. Now, I know that's not a lot, but she was at the top of the apartment complex and if her belly was the size it was now? Surely she would be winded on this trip a few more weeks down the road.

"You should proba—"

She held her hand out to her side, angled back toward me without actually turning to address me. "Save it."

My brows lifted on their own accord, I swear it, at her abrupt dismissal of what I was going to say. "You don't even—"

Mia stopped in front of a door and turned toward me. "I said. Save it."

Well-fucking-then.

I stopped beside her and crossed my arms over my chest. Fine. I wouldn't say it. Yet.

She turned back to her door and unlocked it, stepping inside and holding the door for me. I took the door from her on my own way through and she moved away, toeing out of her shoes. Moving them with her toes, she placed them along the wall and hung her keys on a peg, putting her clutch in a small basket attached to the bar the peg was on.

"I'm going to change into something more comfortable. Just... Sit somewhere." She waved her hand dismissively as she walked away from me and like the involuntary brow raise a little bit ago, my lips were twitching to grin.

I let the door close behind me and bent down to untie my dress shoes, placing them near the shoes Mia set aside. They were next to a pair of running shoes, a nicer pair of sandals, and a pair of those plastic flip flops you could buy for less than five bucks.

Deciding to take a look around, I pocketed my hands and moved quietly through her place. There was a small bathroom and laundry room, and the next room I passed through was a living room area and one of the smallest kitchens I had ever seen.

The place couldn't be much bigger than five hundred square feet. I wondered what she was paying for little digs like this.

Which had me wondering what it was, exactly, she did for a living.

Which, of course, had me curious about how that would all work out once she had the baby.

Fuck. This train of thought I had where Mia was concerned fucking baffled me.

It looked like the nicest piece of furniture in her apartment, and by that, I mean more expensive than twenty dollars apiece, was her couch. I went over to the sectional and sat down, surprised to realize it was extremely comfortable.

I mean...it was bright turquoise, but it was comfortable.

I sat forward, my forearms on my knees, as I waited for her to come back out. I wasn't a lady, but I couldn't think of a reason why her slacks and shirt were uncomfortable and why she had to change. It wasn't like she'd been in them all that long.

She arrived to the restaurant, barfed in the restroom, and left. Not that much time in her clothes.

Then again, she did barf, and was pressed against the restroom wall...

I couldn't help but grin at the memory.

So yeah, maybe that's why she wanted to change. Bathroom walls were dirty. Her panties probably were, too.

When a door opened at the other end of the room, I looked up to see Mia emerge, this time in cotton shorts and a dark t-shirt that hugged her stomach. Her crazy curls were pulled back from her face now, but I only glanced at them quickly before dropping my gaze back to her stomach.

Mia stretched at the bottom hem of her shirt. "They're getting too tight, sorry," she grumbled. Barefoot, she padded past me into the kitchen to grab a bottle of water, then moved back toward me only to stop at the counter seating area. She placed her bottle of water on the counter and pulled out a stool to sit facing me, but she didn't say anything.

I tried to work on getting my mad back, but I couldn't

manage to find any anger as I looked at her sitting there in front of me.

"Were you going to tell me?" There. I would start with that.

She stared at me a moment too long, and I had my answer. No, she hadn't been planning on it.

"I was going to try," she said instead.

I nodded a few times, my eyes locked with hers. She looked uncomfortable but I gave the girl props, she kept eye contact.

"You should—" I started, but she spoke at the same time, "Look, I was—"

We both stopped and stared at one another before Mia sat up a little straighter in her chair.

"I was going to try telling you. I know that's not a good enough answer, but I was going to try. I'm sorry I didn't tell you the first night who I was. I should have. It was childish of me not to tell you, just as it was childish of me to want to be with you for a night."

Well, I wouldn't say *childish*…

"By the time I found out I was pregnant, I was already three months along. Conor, it took me three weeks to try and talk to you, and even that I failed at. I just…" she shrugged her shoulders and looked down at her lap.

I didn't have the anger in me any longer. To be honest, I'm not sure it ever was true anger. When I found out I took her virginity, I was angry, sure, but more at myself. Omitting the truth is lying, yeah, but I probably could have handled her better afterward. And when she walked into the restaurant earlier, it wasn't so much anger as it was *shock* at learning the woman I had fought to get out of my head was a girl I had known when I was a kid, and that she was obviously pregnant with my child.

"What have you been up to, Mia?" I asked. The shock on her face was comical. It was not the direction she was thinking I would go, I was sure.

She contorted her face a few times as she worked on spitting out words, but finally she settled on, "I teach?"

"Is that a question, or is that what you do?"

Mia nodded. "I do. I teach. Second grade."

"So that's what, seven and eight year olds?"

She nodded again.

"How long?"

"I just finished my first school year."

"You get decent benefits?"

She nodded but shrugged as well. "If you're asking about the baby, Conor, I said I was going to be fine." Unlike the previous time she told me this, her voice held no bite.

I shifted in my seat and squinted my eyes ever so slightly. "Do you *want* me in the baby's life?"

I don't know why her answer mattered, but it did. I would have been fine going through my days, not knowing I'd fathered a kid. But knowing there was a kid out there that was mine? I'm not so sure I could do it and not have any sort of contact with it.

"I don't need you in the baby's life, no."

"That wasn't the question though."

"Conor, I don't know you anymore. I can't make that kind of decision. I don't know if there's a good guy under that front you put on at the bar, or if that front is really just you."

"Then ask me something." It caught me off guard, but I wanted her to know who I was. I wanted her to have that knowledge so she could make that decision. Granted, I was surprisingly afraid she would learn that what I put on for show at the bar was really just classic Conor O'Gallagher.

I found myself wanting to know if I could be the good guy who got the girl. Crazy as that fucking sounded.

Mia frowned at me but she didn't move from her spot. I could see the wheels turning behind her eyes. She leaned to her side so she could rest her arm on the counter, her head in her hand, as she scratched at the side of her head. Her eyes remained on me as she thought. "This is awkward."

"Anything, Mia." I leaned back to appear more casual, slouched against her couch with my arms thrown over the back, when casual and carefree were the last two things I felt inside.

Nervous.

Anxious.

Not worthy.

Those were pretty forefront in my mind.

Not to add the confusion of why those things were there.

"Well..." She sat up and rocked in her seat, as if to find a better position. Her eyes were fixed to my chest but moved up to my eyes. "I guess, what have you been up to the last few years? Just taking over the bar?"

"Yeah and no. I bought it from the parents and Rory and I worked on the remodel before opening the doors again."

"Did you go to school?"

I lifted my brow. I remember the day I left for college; it was probably the last time I'd seen a little Mia. "You know I did."

"Well, did you *finish* school, then?"

I nodded. "Business," I said, guessing her next question. I leaned forward again.

"Any serious relationships?"

I shook my head no.

Her brows rose. "None at all?"

I shook my head again. "Nope."

"So you really do just take a random woman up to your place at night. Every night?"

I didn't think lying to her would be a good answer. "Most nights."

"If we do this...co-parenting thing...that stops with the baby." She crossed her arms under her ample chest. "I don't care what you do in your free time, but you don't bring women up when you have the baby."

"I wouldn't." It was my turn to shift in my seat.

"How often are you willing to be away from the bar? You're there all the time now, aren't you?"

I nodded. "Usually, yeah, but I can take time off. What are you thinking? Do you need, want...someone to go to appointments with you?"

She shook her head. "Oh! No, not that. I was talking about when you'd have the baby."

Again, I nodded. Made sense. "I would, you know, go to appointments with you, if you wanted."

"No, that's ok." Mia's smile was forced. "Um. So yeah. What do you… How do you want to do this, I guess?"

"What do you mean?"

"Do we do this civilly between us, do we get lawyers?" She scoffed to herself. "Well, lawyers are probably a good idea, regardless."

"How about we just take it a day at a time?"

Mia swallowed and nodded. "Ok." Her eyes widened briefly and she smiled. "Do you maybe, do you want to feel the baby?"

"Like, touch your stomach?"

"The baby's really active right now. You might not be able to feel it as much as I can, but you might be able to. You know, if you wanted."

Did I want to? Kind of, actually, yeah. It was some weird fucking shit, though.

But this was the most open Mia had been all night and I was going to grab on to that olive branch. I pulled to a stand, rubbing my suddenly wet palms on my pants, and walked the short distance to where she sat. I pushed the sleeves of my shirt up a little more just as I reached her.

Mia reached out a hand and grabbed my wrist. I had to refrain from jumping at the contact. It was electrical, and fuck if I knew what that was about.

She guided my hand to the swell of her stomach and my palm touched just as something pushed from the other side.

Well, not something. Our kid.

Our kid.

I just felt our kid.

And suddenly I wanted nothing more than to be in this kid's life.

And in Mia's.

I would find a way to be in Mia's life, more than just as the father of her child.

For the first time, I wanted forever.

CHAPTER NINE

CONOR

I probably stood there for another five minutes, my hand in one spot on Mia's belly.

She'd ask, "Did you feel that one?" every time she felt a push or a kick, and I found I was disappointed that I only felt a few of the movements she felt.

Her hand was still on my wrist and she guided my hand to the top of the swell. "What about there?"

I tried to focus on my hand and what was beneath it, but I kept fighting my eyes from searching over her face.

This Mia was certainly a grown up Mia from my childhood.

The Mia then was, like Rory and I called her earlier, pudgy. She'd been a little rounder than most of the kids, but she was a laugher. She laughed and she smiled, and as much as I hated Bren and Mia hanging around, there may have been a few days I said no to a party or something just so I could hang out in the backyard with my kid sister and her tagalong friend.

When their friendship ended, I had already left for college, so not seeing her again after that point wasn't something I dwelled on. She was eight years younger than me, and my kid sister's once friend. She'd been a blip on my radar.

It was easy to see how I didn't recognize her back in March. She still had the crazy hair and the eyes that looked like they could see right through you, but she had grown up into quite the beautiful woman. No, she wasn't flashy like many of the women I spent my time with, but still, there was something about her.

Mia's gaze was down on our hands the entire time, and finally she glanced up to see me watching her. Her face flushed and she bit on her lower lip, much like she did again and again that night in March.

We had made good leeway tonight, came pretty far from the argument at the restaurant, and I shouldn't want to overstep the line.

But I wanted to.

And because I wasn't one to take too big of a step back, I did what I wanted.

As I slid my hand down the swell and over to her hip, I leaned down so I could press my lips to hers. Before meeting her lips though, I paused long enough to let her pull back.

But Mia didn't pull back.

No, no she didn't.

She leaned up. I could feel her hip tense as she pushed to stand on her stool just enough to make that contact, and then relax as I met her and followed her back down as she sat. Putting my other hand to her face, I kept my lips against hers light and the kiss slow. What I really wanted was to lift her up and find her bed, toss her down and fuck her senseless, but there was the kid between us now.

Shit, how did that work?

Mia pulled back and frowned up at me, so I mirrored her frown. "What?"

She shifted in her seat. "Don't start something you have no intention of finishing. Don't...*kiss* me because you feel like it will give you...I don't know, *leeway* with me. Just..." She maneuvered to stand and squeezed past me, her baby belly brushing against me. "We can't kiss, Conor. We just. We can't."

She was moving away, but fuck, I didn't want her to. I reached with both hands, grabbing onto her hips, and pulling her back as I moved forward. When I rocked my erection against her, she gasped lightly.

"Give me a chance," I whispered into her ear, rubbing my chin just under it.

Her laugh was cold. "Give you a chance? Geez, Conor, why would I want to do that?" She looked at me over her shoulder, but didn't move away from where I was pressed into her back. "This is probably just some...I don't know, fetish or something. You're curious about *fucking* a pregnant girl and—"

Everything kind of drowned out after she used the term 'fucking'. That's what I did, yes, but to hear it coming out of Mia's mouth? Can't say I liked it too much.

"—eventually you'll just get sick of me, of us, and you'll leave. Sorry if I don't want to play that game."

With my hands on her hips, I turned her to face me. Her face was still flushed, or rather, it was flushed again, and her eyes were wild. But her lower lip was trembling again.

"Look. This is new for me. I'm guessing it's new for you too. I don't see any chicklets running around." I lifted my brows, waiting for her to challenge me in the way she did. When she didn't, I continued. "I can't promise next week. Fuck, I can't promise tomorrow. But I want," I shrugged and swallowed. Shit these words were hard. "I'd like to try."

She stared at me like I grew two heads. Fuck, maybe I did.

"But...I mean..." Mia stumbling over her words was kind of cute. She was flustered and it was more than evident. "That's not *you* though, Conor. I'm sorry, but you're a flirt. And while, yeah, flirting isn't necessarily the end all, you don't just flirt to flirt. You flirt to get laid."

Lady had a point. "Just let me try." I don't know why this mattered so much to me, but it did.

Mia shook her head, raised her brows, and I'm pretty sure she rolled her eyes, all in one move that my sister did all too well. It meant she'd fold. It meant—

"Whatever. I guess you can try. But!" She held up a finger between us. "If you're serious, you are going to be monogamous."

I grinned crookedly. "So that means we'll be having sex."

Her hand shot out so fast, hitting my chest before I could stop her, but it didn't stop the laugh that burst out of me.

"I haven't decided yet. Just...one day at a time, Conor." She wiggled her hips from my hands, trying to pull away, but I just pulled her closer. Fucking belly of hers wouldn't allow her to be as close as I wanted her, but that was ok. I'd deal.

"Seal the deal?" I asked down to her, and her brows creased yet again. I let go of a hip so I could rub my thumb over the ridges there. "You're going to get stuck, you keep doing that."

"I just...I don't *know* you Conor, and this?" She waved a hand between us in the miniscule space between our chests, "this isn't the Conor I've been watching."

"You said you'd give me a chance."

"I don't want you to resent me."

"I couldn't resent you. And you said you'd give me a chance. Day at a time." I slid my hand to the back of her head, grabbing her bun-contained curls in my hand and pulling her head back ever so slightly. "Give me my chance," I whispered, before lowering my lips to hers once again.

Now that I started kissing again, I couldn't seem to stop. At least, I couldn't seem to stop kissing Mia. Her lips were a drug. Her responses, a drug. She gave me a fucking high, and I couldn't help but want to stay on the upper she gave me. I squeezed her hip under my hand before moving back to grab a handful of her ass, causing Mia to moan under my mouth.

I let go of her hair so I could put my other hand under her ass, lifting her up. Automatically, her legs wrapped around me but she pulled her mouth away from mine, eyes wide.

"I'm too heavy for you!" She didn't make any moves to get down, though.

"Shut up, you're fine," I told her. Maybe 'shut up' wasn't the best word choice, but it was what I had. "We're going to your room. Objections?" I moved so I could press my lips against the column of her neck, biting and sucking here and there until I left a mark near her collar bone.

Mia's head dropped back with that move, but did not object to my statement, so I moved us toward the room she came out of a short while ago in new clothes.

The night had started to creep in, leaving her room dark. I blindly hit the wall with one hand, finding the light switch, dousing her bedroom in light.

I didn't have time to look around the place. I spotted what I wanted, where I wanted to go, and I moved us to her bed.

Thank fucking God she didn't say anything about the light. I wasn't having that argument right now. I resisted throwing her down on the bed, because of the baby and all, and moved up on her mattress on my knees, lowering her back gently once I reached the middle.

Her bed was likely a queen, but felt like a fucking twin compared to my own luxury bed. Far too small.

I pulled back and immediately started to tug down on her shorts. "Are you able to stay on your back?" I asked as I went to task. I didn't bother stopping as she answered.

"Right now, yes. In a few weeks, probably not." Her voice was husky and slightly breathless and I had to fight a grin of satisfaction. I did that to her.

I leaned back to completely take off her shorts, not at all surprised to find she was in those cotton underwear. Maybe I could talk her into lace or silk someday.

Hm. Yeah. Someday.

Depositing her shorts on the floor beside her bed, I moved my hands up to the hem of her shirt. The plain cotton was surprisingly thick. I was a fan of soft, vintage style tees myself, but to each his, or her, own. My thumbs hooked under the hem and I pulled the fabric up, exposing her stomach inch by inch.

My eyes darted up to Mia's to catch her reaction and I was semi-surprised to find her eyes on mine already, her lip between her teeth, as if she were afraid of my response. I moved my eyes back down to her stomach, which was stretched and taut.

I will admit—it was a fucking powerful feeling knowing she held a baby in her stomach and that I put it there. Yeah, Mia and I had some way to go, but I wasn't kidding when I said I wanted to try.

Inch by inch, I exposed more of her stomach. Her belly button ring was no longer in, and her belly button itself was starting to pop out. Unable to resist, I bent down to press my lips to her stomach as I pushed her shirt up to her tits. I pressed my lips over and over again to the swell of her stomach and chuckled when the kid pressed against my lips. It was a soft, fluttery feeling, but I felt it and Goddamn, it made me feel like fucking Superman.

I sat back on my knees and pulled her up to sit so I could finish pulling her shirt off. I groaned out loud when her breasts were freed from the shirt, showing she wasn't wearing a bra. God fucking damn.

Her tits were indeed larger than I remembered, and her nipples...

Fuck, her nipples were huge and dark and begging to be in my mouth.

I peeled the shirt over her head, tossing it to the ground at the same time I sucked one of her nipples into my mouth. Mia's hands were in my hair, holding me close, as I sucked, running my tongue over the hardening peak. I licked, pulled back, licked again, sucked her into my mouth where I bit down gently and played with the peaked nipple with my tongue. I put my other hand over her cotton underwear, holding my palm over her. I could feel her wet heat through the cotton, her panties already wet.

I pushed Mia back gently to lay once again, and moved my mouth to give her other tit the attention it deserved, all while moving my lower hand up just enough to slide under the band of her cotton panties, finding the goods that lie underneath.

When my fingers brushed over her clit, I sucked hard on her nipple, eliciting a gasp from Mia. She was fucking soaked, her wetness making the glide over her clit slippery and easy. I rubbed quick circles there, moved my fingers back and forth over the nub, too, before sliding down and finding the source of all that wet gloriousness. With ease, I slipped two fingers into her, no preamble, no hesitation. My fingers moved in easily up to my top knuckle, and I slowly began to pull my fingers in and out.

Mia's hips moved restlessly below me as I continued my ministrations on her tit, going back and forth, showing equal attention to both.

"Oh my God, Conor." Her body tensed all around me and I could feel the telltale pulses saying she was about to come. I moved my mouth to hers, speaking against her lips.

"Let it go. Let go, Mia. Just let go." I moved my fingers in her faster, curling up into her walls, letting my palm hit her clit and add more pressure. Soon enough, Mia was crashing through her high, her arched back pressing that baby belly into my stomach.

I kept my mouth on hers, gently nibbling at her lips until she was finally through with her quiet moaning. *I need to get this girl to be more vocal*, I thought offhandedly.

Rather than give her reprieve to breathe, I crushed my mouth to hers, sweeping my tongue inside. This kiss was fevered and Mia was an active participant, her tongue and teeth clashing with my own. Her hands were in my hair, down my back, grabbing my still clothed ass. And my fingers were still lodged way up deep in her pussy.

She shuddered and bit down on my lip, not so gently, mind you, as I slowly pulled my fingers out. I left her with one more kiss before moving to stand beside her bed. In no time at all, I was out of my clothes and on my side beside her.

I turned her to her side to face me, one hand under my head so I could look down at her and my other hand moved to rest on her hip. For the first time since losing my virginity at fourteen years old, I didn't have a fucking clue where to start with a woman.

Forward, backward, fuck, upside down? What would be best for Mia?

Apparently I wasn't going to have to think long. Mia had her hands between us before I could even try to ask. Those fingers of hers were wrapped around my huge, aching cock and shortly after, my dirty bird lifted her leg to drape over my hip, angling her hips so she could brush the head of my cock over her folds.

Fuck, yes.

MIA

For a sex god, Conor was thinking too much. I could practically hear the wheels turning in his head.

I was probably a fool for wanting this with him, wanting to

see if he could do the commitment thing, but every girl wanted to live out their childhood crush. I wasn't asking him to marry me, for goodness sake.

I moved so I could angle his cock where I needed it to be. Before I could attempt to sink down on him though, Conor rested his head down on the pillow, using that arm to pull my upper body in close, and slammed up into me. I let out a breathless moan and pushed my nose into his chest, squeezing my eyes shut at the tight intrusion.

"So fucking tight," Conor murmured into my ear. "God, I missed this tight fucking pussy. Didn't realize I could until this moment. So fucking right." His hips thrusted against mine and he held onto my leg that was over his side.

I loved that he talked dirty. It wasn't surprising, no, but it was just enough incentive to get me close to flying over the edge again. I moaned, greedy little moans, as he moved his hips in and against mine.

"Use your words, baby girl. Use your words. Tell me." His voice was in my ear, followed by kisses raining over my cheekbone. "Give me the words. Harder, faster. Anything. Tell me, Mia."

My only sexual partner had been Conor, and toys certainly didn't ask you to talk to them. I was so used to being quiet that even the thought of using the words was foreign to me.

When I didn't comply, Conor pushed his hips up into me and did some hip twist or another that nearly had me seeing stars. "You like that, Mia? Tell me. Tell me you like it, baby girl."

"Yes," I managed, shakily at best.

"Yes what?"

He was going to pull them out of me. He did the move yet again and I had to close my eyes against the onslaught of pleasure.

"God, yes, I like that."

"Conor works fine," he chuckled against my forehead. "Or Con. But I guess God works."

Before I could give him a sassy reply, my body was once

again shattering around him. My God, what the hell did this man eat for breakfast? I had an idea of how often he practiced his moves, so I didn't really care to have that question answered, but really, the man was phenomenal in bed.

My jaw was dropped as I went through the waves of pleasure. My breath held. My eyes squeezed tight.

"Talk to me," he pressed. He flipped onto his back, pulling me on top of him. I had to press up on my forearms to be comfortable, baby belly and all, but my body was still spasming and the act took more energy than I had in me.

"Give me something, Mia." His cock was still sliding in and out of me, slowly as if he was having a hard time pushing his girth through the pulsing muscles.

Without thinking, I said the first word that came to mind. "Fuck." But the word wasn't as nice and quick and easy as one would think a one syllable word to be. Oh no. I drew that damn word out for a good five seconds, which earned me a chuckle from below me.

My body was finally slowing off its ebb, just enough that I could glare down at him, but he took no mind to the look.

Nope, if anything, he sensed the energy was well and gone from me and he sat up straight, hugging me close, his knees bent, and began mercilessly pounding up into me, finding his own release. I wrapped my arms tight around his neck, holding him as close as I could, as he pushed his forehead down into my shoulder.

"Fuck!"

I have to say, his was a bit more exciting than mine was, all loud and full of passion. Who knew Conor had it in him? His body pulled tight, straining under and around me, and I could feel every muscle in his upper back as his cock jerked inside me, leaving behind warm wetness. It was something I hadn't felt the first time we were together, regardless of the broken condom. It was...

Interesting.

We stayed locked around one another for a number of minutes, as my breath finally calmed down and his body started to do the same.

Conor finally lifted his head and looked at me, his blue eyes set and determined, but with a warmth I wasn't prepared for. "You ok?"

I nodded.

"The baby ok?"

I couldn't help but grin. "You can't hurt the baby with sex, Conor."

"Well, I know, but..." Holy hell, Conor had a bashful side. I could see a slight blush rise behind his bearded cheeks. I grabbed said cheeks and brought his forehead to my smiling lips, pressing a kiss there, before pushing against his shoulders to try and stand.

I pushed myself up, biting on my lip when his cock dislodged from me, and stood in front of him. Belatedly I realized where his face would be when I did so, and before I could try to walk off the edge of the bed, Conor's hands were at my ass, pulling me close to his mouth.

"Conor, no!" I put my hands on his head. "It's...*messy*."

"Fuck messy," he murmured against my mound. Before I knew it, his tongue was between my pussy lips, lapping up the both of us. I had to brace my hands on the wall behind the bed to keep from falling.

I mentioned it before that I was a sexual being, even if I hadn't had sex, but these pregnancy hormones were no joke. Before long, I was coming against his face. "Jesus, Conor," I said around a quiet moan.

"You're getting better."

I frowned and stepped back, almost falling and having to brace myself with a hand on his head. "Excuse me?" I was getting *better*? Was that some offhanded remark about my inexperience? Where the fuck was he going with that comment? Was he fucking kidding me?

And then he had the gall to fucking laugh at me! *And* slap my ass?

Fucking jerk.

I stomped off the bed, as gingerly as I could without falling on my ass and making more of a show than I intended, and headed toward the bathroom. My small apartment didn't have the luxury of a bathroom attached to the bedroom. I had to stomp naked through my apartment to get to the bathroom at the front of the space.

"Mia!" Conor yelled after me, but I kept going.

And shit, cue the water works.

God fucking damn, the hormones!

"Mia. Mia, baby girl. Stop. Stop, Mia!" His voice was drawing near. Not hard to do. It wasn't as if there was a ton of square footage between the bed and the bathroom. He reached for my arm and I swung around on him so fast, he probably thought he was seeing the Exorcist.

"You're a jerk, Conor O'Gallagher! I don't know why I agreed to give you a chance." I brought my free hand up to my face. "I'm so fucking *stupid*!"

Conor was fucking laughing again as he brought me in for a hug. I was confused and pissed, and my nose was pressed against his chest and fuck him for still smelling good, even with the lingering scent of sex between us.

"You're misreading the situation, Mia." The smile was evident in his voice, the bastard. "I meant, you were getting better at *vocalizing*." He drew the word out and it kind of made me feel, well, stupid.

"Oh." I dipped my chin down and Conor took the opportunity to press his lips to the back of my head.

"Why don't you clean up," he said against my head, "and then we'll continue to talk, kay?"

I nodded and finally moved my head so I could look at him again. "Ok."

He had the audacity to grin at me again, the crinkles beside his eyes deepening. I merely lifted my brows and pointed at him before turning and finishing the few steps to the bathroom, closing myself in the room, locking Conor out.

And then I grinned wide, my lower lip between my teeth, and refrained from doing a little dance with myself.

CHAPTER TEN

CONOR

After pulling my briefs and slacks back on, I may have snooped around her room a bit. Mia had semi-mentioned she had toys and I was curious as all fucking get out as to what she had. Hands in my pockets, I walked around gingerly, slowly. On the other side of the bed was where I hit the jackpot. Plugged into the wall was a vibrating wand, and in a basket nearby was a freaking dildo and this other compact looking thing. I crouched down to pick up the pink device and turned it over in my hands. It had a hollow nub at the top. I put my finger over it and found the on-switch, chuckling when the nub started to pulse and squeeze my finger.

I knew she liked her tits and clit worked on, but I definitely wanted to see this one in action someday.

I turned the device off and put it back in the basket, and headed back into the living room where I could hear the shower running.

I lounged on Mia's comfy-ass couch, waiting for her to get out of the bathroom. For all I knew, I was going to be here for a while, Mia being female and all, but rather than be uncomfortable in her space...

I found I enjoyed the peacefulness it brought to me.

I could still hear the shower running behind the bathroom door and imagined the water dripping down her tits, falling off her tight peaks. Soap running down and over the swell of her belly, disappearing between her thighs.

I shifted in my seat and adjusted myself. Getting hard right now wouldn't do me any good.

I squeezed myself through the cotton and polyester blend of

my slacks. Now that I started, I couldn't turn off the images of Mia playing in my head, imagining what she looked like in the shower. Those curls of hers relaxed and around her shoulders. Her eyelashes wet from the stream of the shower.

Her pink lips brighter from her constant nibbling on them.

The door to the bathroom opened, pulling me from my daydream. I was hard as a fucking rock under my hand and I groaned to myself, knowing that when I pulled my hand away, I was going to have major tentage.

Mia, bless her fucking sweet heart, stepped out of the bathroom wrapped in just a white towel, took one glance at my lap, and shook her head before walking past me toward her bedroom.

What I wanted to do was follow her and beat off to her changing, but at the same time, I really did want to prove that I could be in this for the long haul, with or without the sexual benefits.

Beneficial as they were.

I stood instead, pushing my hands in my pockets, and turned to study the photographs adorning her walls. I was surprised to find they were all landscape photos; not a single one had a person in them.

When I heard her walk back into the room, I asked without turning, "How are your parents?"

"They're good. They still live in the old neighborhood. Different house, though."

Mia moved to stand beside me and I looked down to see she was in the same cotton shorts as earlier, but a different tee, this one a little looser. Her hair was actually pretty long when it was wet, and with it straight from her shower, she almost looked like a different person.

I liked her crazy curls better though, I decided. It was more Mia.

"You don't have pictures of them."

She laughed lightly. "Ah, they're all on a hard drive. Or my phone. You know, the digital age."

I nodded because I actually did understand that. The only

picture I had around of my parents was in the bar, from when they opened O'Gallaghers, and it was right next to a picture of Rory, Bren, and I at the re-opening.

Mia moved to sit on the couch where I had previously been, her hands clasped between her knees. The move pressed her tits together and I had to fight the onslaught of another fucking erection. Good God, the woman did things to me.

"So what now?" she asked softly.

Wasn't that the real question? What now?

"Well," I said on a sigh, my hands still in my pockets, I looked down at her and shrugged. "I'm not entirely sure. We already agreed to be exclusive while we're trying this out. Is there, like, a time limit or something?"

"Do you want a time limit?" Mia tilted her head toward her shoulder, her eyes inquisitive and on mine.

Did I want a time limit? Well, no. Not really. "I think I want to give this a good, real try," I told her instead. "Dates. I'll go to appointments with you. We figure out what's best for us and the baby."

Mia patted the couch beside her and I moved to sit next to her. "I'm kind of afraid that sex might cloud judgment," she told me. "Or really if I'm being honest, the lack of multiple partners for you."

I had an idea and as much as it baffled the hell out of me, it was going to throw Mia for a loop. "Then we don't have it."

She looked at me skeptically. "Seriously." Her voice was deadpanned and her brows were lifted up to her hairline.

I nodded a few times. "Yeah. Why not?"

"Because you're Conor O'Gallagher, that's why."

"I can go without sex." Even I could hear the slight disbelief in my voice. No, I really hadn't ever put myself on a celibacy streak, but I could do it. I knew I could.

Mia shifted in her spot and turned toward me, her leg folded to the side and between the two of us. Her clasped hands sat in the spot between her legs, in front of her pussy, her arms bracketing her belly. With her leg up, the cotton of her shorts stretched and I could almost, *almost*, see the land of glory.

She lifted a hand and snapped her fingers in front of my face. "Up here, Romeo."

I lifted my eyes to hers and offered her a coy grin. "I can," I repeated.

"Let's just say, I don't know, a month."

"Of us trying?"

"Of no sex. Keep up, Conor."

Shit. I could do that. A month was nothing. "Alright. Deal."

"We don't have to go on dates, either. Maybe just dinner now and then."

"I'm taking you out on a date, Mia."

"Maybe just lunch after an appointment, then."

"Mia. I'm taking you out on a date."

"You're stubborn."

"Kettle, meet pot." I reached out to take her hand. "I'm taking you out to dinner. I'm going to your appointments. And in one month, we'll decide if sex is going on the table or not."

"You mean you want to *have* sex on the table." Mia, the sass, grinned.

"I think you're the one who's going to have an issue with the no sex clause," I said around a laugh.

Mia just shook her head, still smiling though. "Nah. I've only had one partner. And you're good, Con, you are, but…"

"You know you like it. Don't even try saying you don't. I'm better than your toys."

Her brows went up. "How do you know about my toys?"

"Well, you eluded to them once, but I may have found them."

Her brows stayed raised, but her eyes widened to join them. "You *snooped*?"

"I was changing and they were…just there." I grinned wide and reached up to scratch my chin.

Mia jerked her hand from mine, only so she could put both her hands over her face. "Oh my God, this is embarrassing."

I reached for her hands and pulled them down. "Nothing to be embarrassed about." I leaned in to kiss her lips once. I was starting to regret not kissing her the first time I had her in my bed. "It's sexy as hell. We're gonna play with them in a month."

Mia's devilish side must have wanted to play because, while she was still blushing, she bit down on that lip of hers and said, "We could always play with them tonight. And tomorrow night. We just can't have actual sex."

I really liked the way this woman thought, but, "No." I shook my head. "We are going to abstain one-hundred percent, Mia."

She pouted and it was fucking adorable. "I don't think you understand how pregnancy hormones work."

"You're all hot and bothered, yeah, I get that." I reached forward to brush one of her tightening curls behind her ear. "But I want to do this right."

"What's the male version of a cock tease?"

Shaking my head, I turned on the couch, pulling Mia with me, so I could lay back. Mia's ass stayed between my legs, snug up to my covered cock, and I pulled her down to lay on me. I wrapped my arms around her shoulders, holding her in place. "You'll survive."

Mia rotated her shoulders so she could rub herself against me. "But will you?"

"Barely," I groaned.

She turned, much to my displeasure, and pulled herself up to her knees, propping her hands on my bare stomach. "I don't want you to resent me, Conor." The words were said softly.

I reached up for her face, pulling her back down, and spoke against her lips, before kissing her. "I don't think I could, Mia."

CHAPTER ELEVEN

ONE MONTH LATER

MIA

The past month flew by.

Conor had invited me to a wedding in Wisconsin and I'd been shocked when I learned it was for an NHL player. Apparently Conor and the groom had become fast friends through the bar.

True to his word, Conor didn't try any frisky business with me, and that weekend away was the first time he and I stayed in a bed together since the night of our talk. I was semi-expecting, shoot, I was hoping, he would try something, *touch* something, but other than holding me through the night, his hands didn't make any moves. If I had to guess, I would think he just liked keeping his hands on my belly to try to catch the baby moving, not the actual touching *me* part.

After that weekend though, Conor started staying the night.

Every night.

Said he liked to sleep next to me.

And that his California King was too damn big without me in it. That he'd take my little queen sized bed with me in it any day of the week.

Which baffled me because I personally would take the space of his large bed any day of the week. I was starting to get super warm at night and had to pee at least once a night, if not twice. Having Conor's big, burly form wrapped around me kind of became a pain some nights.

Conor cut back on his time at the bar, too. Said he wanted to spend more time with me, and that Rory and Brenna were more than capable of handling the day to day operations. We also may have had a slightly heated discussion about it a week or two ago.

He still tended bar Thursday through Sunday, and still wore a kilt for ladies' night, but swore he didn't take any ladies up to the apartment with him.

Which I believed full-heartedly.

I mean, he always crawled into my bed thirty minutes after bar-close so unless he was doing magic quickies…

More than that, though, I was growing to trust him.

He still had his cocky ways with his fast grins, but when he was with me, he was with me one-thousand percent. We learned a lot about one another over the last month too, catching up on the last fifteen years.

I also started back at school two weeks ago. While Conor slept until noon, I went off to work. He would sometimes stop by the school during my lunch break and eat a brown bag lunch with me in my classroom.

Seeing Conor in a little green chair did serious things to my heart.

But finally, we reached a month.

Today.

And I was newly two weeks into the third trimester and if I hit the 'don't touch me with that thing' phase after spending the last four weeks in sexual need-but-not-getting, I was going to…

I don't know, but Conor wouldn't be very happy.

I considered going to his apartment, but he was at the bar and he'd know something was up. As it was, he was only working the lunch crowd today, leaving the crazy Saturday night to Stone and Rory.

He'd be back to my place in an hour. I wasn't planning anything extravagant, and I didn't have any fancy teddies or anything. It was hard to find something and feel super sexy with this belly. Thankfully, my belly hadn't done too much growing the last few weeks; at least, I didn't think so. Ask Conor, and it grew leaps and bounds. I was the one sporting it, though, and I didn't really notice too much of a difference.

But my belly button officially popped out. And there was that line down my belly. And the stretch marks. They were all things these days.

Like I said. Hard to feel sexy.

I did order lacy boy shorts and a bra for the occasion, but wasn't planning on putting them on until right before Conor walked through my door.

We had found an easy rhythm for us as a couple. There wasn't any talk about what was going to happen after today, being the end of that first month, but I was comfortable with the thought this was happening, that this could be a long-term thing. That we could co-parent and everything would be right in Baby O'Gallagher's world.

We hadn't talked names, but we did discuss that the baby would take Conor's surname. It only made sense to me. However, the closer we got to D-day, the more we should probably start considering first names.

With a sigh, I walked back to my room to be sure everything was in place.

CONOR

I never realized how exhausting not having sex could be. Every night I slept wrapped up in Mia. Every night, I went to bed with a case of blue balls worse than the night before.

But while I went to sleep uncomfortable, I found myself waking up more than comfortable. This thing between Mia and me had an easy rhythm and, as much as I didn't want to be the owner of the idea, I really think that the no-sex thing worked in our favor.

It was no secret that I liked sex, that before Mia coming back into my life, the longest I went without it was maybe two days. And I usually made up for those off days when I got back in the sack. Being with Mia, and not being able to sink into her wet heat, had its challenges, sure, but I think I decided I liked myself better as a person, and it reinforced that I could do the co-parenting and monogamy thing long-term.

Earlier this month, I brought her to Caleb and Sydney's wedding with me. I enjoyed showing her off, her standing at my side and my hand covering her belly.

These days, Rory teased her like he teased Brenna. Bren and Mia... I was pretty sure they were on good terms now, too. Neither talked to me about what they talked about to one another, but things were easy all around where Mia and my family were concerned.

Today, Stone showed up to the bar an hour early, but rather than head to Mia's, I went back to the office to try and do some bookkeeping that was due to be finished tomorrow.

Mia didn't know it, but right after I found out we were having a kid, I bought a copy of that book, *The Expectant Father*. I devoured the months we were already past, curious about what Mia had been through, and then I fucking studied the hell out of the months to come. When I got to her apartment one Wednesday morning after close, something she said triggered a piece of information I read. I let her go back to sleep, pissy as she'd been, and in the morning I made sure to wake up with her and her alarm and we talked about me cutting down on my hours.

I owned the fucking bar. I made enough money managing the place that bartending wasn't necessary. So we made a compromise that I'd work Thursday and Friday nights, Saturday afternoons, and leave Sunday for bookkeeping. That way when the kid was here, we'd have more flexibility once Mia went back to work.

As for tonight...

If I had my way, I was going to be up really late and wasn't planning on leaving Mia's arms until *maybe* tomorrow afternoon at the earliest.

We reached our month.

And I had plans for my baby mama.

There was also the fact that *The Expectant Father* mentioned Mia's libido could potentially drop, and I'd be damned if we went a month without sex, a month where right before the vow, Mia was downright *craving* sex, for her to put up the red light because she wasn't feeling it anymore.

I booted up my laptop and while my accounting program loaded, I opened up my email to check on the status of a ring I'd been looking at.

Yeah, yeah, it was definitely too fucking early to talk about marriage, but it was something that had been sitting in the back of my mind since watching Cael get hitched.

Damn internet was slow as fuck today.

I sighed and leaned back in my chair, closing my eyes while I waited.

CHAPTER TWELVE

CONOR

My cock was getting some crazy attention.

What a fucking crazy sex dream, I thought as I started to come to. My book mentioned I may have sex dreams which I thought was fucking bogus. Mia, on the other hand, oh yeah, she was having some crazy sex dreams, but this was a first for me.

Not only could I imagine Mia's hands rubbing up and down my cock, moving my zipper lower over the hardening length, but I could fucking *feel* that shit.

I groaned and shifted, trying to fully wake up, when a giggle that *wasn't* Mia sounded in the room.

My eyes snapped open, my booted feet pushed my chair back as far as I could, and I searched frantically for the intrusion.

Sitting where my feet had been by the desk, was one of our blonde regulars.

She smiled wide up at me. "Hey, Conor. You were so exhausted behind the bar today, I thought I'd give you a little...pick me up."

My heart was pounding, my hands on the arm rests of my chair. My body was fucking paralyzed, trying to figure out what the hell to do. I glanced down and saw my cock nearly completely out of my pants and just as I went to tuck myself in, just as I was going to stand up and order her out of the room...

My office door opened.

And Mia stood there.

Her face fucking fell, and it was a fucking punch to the gut. I thought I was paralyzed before? Everything fucking stood still right then.

I lost my breath, my heart was three times too big for my chest, and the erection I was sporting, the one I was sporting from thoughts of Mia, quickly deflated.

And then Mia turned on her heel, and my world spun into fast forward.

I tucked myself back into my pants quickly, not fucking paying attention to much of anything when I zipped, damn near zipping my fucking cock in the process. Fucking A, that shit hurt!

But it was nothing, fucking *nothing*, compared to the thought that everything I was working for this last month was about to just...

Go *poof*.

"You're not fucking welcome here," I issued to the blonde as I stormed out of the office. She just fucking stood there like a Goddamn doll, not caring about a damn thing.

Fuck.

I should have figured something like this was gonna to happen. I had a fucking reputation! Sooner or later, it was going to get around that I wasn't fucking sleeping around anymore. God-*fucking*-damn.

I peeled around the corner as Mia pushed through the swinging door separating the kitchen from the bar. I ran the length of the kitchen, narrowly dodging my weekend cook at the fryer, and ran through the swinging doors.

"Mia!"

She was close to the door.

If she got through that door, if she got to her car...

Shit, I couldn't think like that.

"Mia!" I lengthened my stride, reaching her just as she got to the front door. I slapped my hand over where the door and jamb met, and put my other hand on her hip.

"Don't *fucking touch me!*" she yelled, twirling around on me. Her yell was hysterical and before I looked into those whiskey eyes I was learning to enjoy so damn much, I knew, I fucking knew, they were going to be filled with tears. And these ones wouldn't be due to pregnancy hormones.

"You were *late*, so I thought I'd check on you. I should have figured you couldn't hold up on your end of the deal. How long, Conor? Huh? How long?" Her words were watery and she refused to look at me, instead looking clear to the side toward the back of the bar where our dart boards were set up.

I took her face in my hands and bent down to her level, forcing her to look at me. When she still refused to move her eyes, I leaned over, blocking her gaze. "Listen to me, Mia." My voice was low, quiet, almost a whisper, but the desperation was more than clear. "I didn't do anything."

Her eyes moved back and forth between mine and she let out a small sob, followed by a hiccup, and shook her head with my hands still on her. "I don't believe you. I don't believe you, Conor. I don't believe you."

"I didn't. I swear to fucking God, Mia, I didn't do anything." I wasn't above begging at this point. I straightened enough so I could press my lips to her forehead. "I fell asleep and woke up and she was there. Fuck, Mia, I thought she was you!"

Mia sniffled and tilted her head down, this time looking at our feet.

Well, she probably really only saw her belly.

God, her belly.

She couldn't walk away. She couldn't.

"She's blonde."

I tried really fucking hard not to laugh at that. Hand to God, I didn't mean to chuckle, but if that was the only thing Mia could come up with, then I knew this was going to be ok.

She swung her head up so fast, she nearly clipped me in the chin, causing me to almost laugh again but the glare in her eyes had me stopping. "She's a *blonde*, Conor. How did you think she was me?"

"I was sleeping, Mia baby." My voice was quiet again. This conversation was for Mia only, not the gawkers who kept glancing over at us. Stone, good man that he was, turned up the baseball game on one TV, and was talking loudly about the latest NHL trades with a couple of the patrons. "Come upstairs with me. Please."

She sniffed again and clenched her jaw. I could see that determined, *stubborn* side trying to win out in my girl but finally she just nodded. "But only because we're making a scene. Which we seem to do so well," she added in a smart-assed, off-handed mumbled way. I didn't bother stopping my chuckle this time.

She stepped out of my hold and skirted around me, heading back toward the doors we both just came barreling out of.

Just before getting there, of course the fucking blonde had to walk through.

I was ready to pull Mia to me, make an announcement to the entire bar that my cock was closed for business, but Mia beat me to the punch.

She pointed at the girl and said through her teeth. "He's mine." Damn, I loved that possessive tone in her voice.

Blonde, stupid assed bitch, just grinned. "He doesn't do seconds, sweetheart. Everyone knows that."

"I don't know if you noticed, but he's done seconds with me. And thirds." That was a great exaggeration on Mia's part, because I'd been sporting a hard dick and blue balls for a month, but the thought was the same.

Mia rubbed her belly and the blonde glanced down, eyes widening as if she only just now noticed the bump Mia was sporting.

It wasn't exactly small.

I reached around Mia and placed my hand on top of hers, rubbing the bump with her. "Just leave her, Mia." The baby kicked under our hands, giving its opinion of the matter as well.

My grin was huge as shit. The kicks and punches were getting stronger. According to my book, it wouldn't be long until Mia and I could watch, without touching, as the baby moved and I was fucking excited as shit for that.

That would be so fucking cool. Weird, but fucking cool.

"Well, when you change your mind," blondie said as she walked away, her eyes full of a promise I had no intention of unwrapping. Ignoring her, I took Mia's hand in mine and we made our way through the kitchen, up the stairs, into my apartment.

"I had a surprise for you," Mia found her voice after I closed the door, locking it behind us.

"What kind of surprise?" I asked, curious.

Her hand still in mine, Mia pulled me to the couch where she turned me and pushed on my stomach until I sat down with a grin. With her lip lower lip locked between her teeth, she moved her feet so she could straddle my legs, hoisting up the lower hem of the cotton dress she wore.

I took her all in, now that there were no outside distractions. Her face was still flushed from the emotion of downstairs, and her voice still had a bit of a quiver in it, but her eyes lost that wildness.

She wore a simple white, cotton dress, but it cut in at her shoulders in the racer-back fashion, leaving her shoulders bare. It also gave the illusion she wasn't wearing a bra, but I knew my woman's tits; she was wearing a bra.

The cotton stretched tight over her belly. Every day, at least that's what it felt like, her belly got a little bit bigger. I loved putting my hands on her and feeling our kid move around inside of her. Through the thicker, soft cotton, I could see where her belly button was.

When Mia woke up last week and saw it had popped out, she cried.

I laughed, yeah, because of her antics, but then I held her, rocked with her, and told her she was beautiful.

Because she was.

This woman with her crazy hair and not-flashy clothes, this woman who sometimes came home from work with marker up and down her arms and glitter in her hair, she was mine.

I focused back on the here and now, trying not to chuckle yet again as Mia attempted to put her knees on the couch beside my ass, to sit on my lap facing me. Unfortunately, our kid was in the way.

Mia growled and pushed against my chest so she could stand again. "It worked in my head."

"I'm telling you, Mia, your belly's growing."

"It's not."

I laughed at her scowl. "Yeah, Mia baby, it is." I spread my knees and pulled her to stand between them. I pressed my lips to her belly in question before lifting the lower hem of her dress. I was guessing her goal was to get naked, so I was only happy to oblige.

Imagine my surprise when the cotton panties I was expecting were actually a pair of lacy boyshorts in a nude color.

"Damn, Mia."

I could never again see another thong and be fine. In the last month, I had my hands on more pairs of thick cotton, thin cotton, bright colored cotton, and black cotton panties, than I ever had before in my life, and I liked it because it was *Mia*. But this lace she pulled out....

"I bought them for today."

I grinned up at her. "Ah, so you were hoping to get lucky on day one of month two."

Finally, she smiled down at me. "Well, yeah. It was your stupid rule."

"Mm," I nodded and, with the fabric of her dress in my fists above the swell of her stomach, I kissed her belly again, this time lips to skin. "But I think I proved myself to you, yeah?"

Mia put a hand on my shoulder and thread her other through my hair, brushing it back gently with a sweet, kind smile on her face. "Yes, Conor."

"And today?"

A look of panic, then insecurity, flashed over her features before she shrugged. "I'm not really sure what to do about that for the future. You have a reputation, you know."

"I'm putting a picture up." It wasn't what I originally thought I was going to say, but it was a great idea. "Next to the picture of my parents, and the one of Bren, Rory and me. You and me. Cael texted me a picture from the wedding."

Mia's brows raised. "You're putting a picture of us up?"
"Yeah, why not? Then the women will see."

She looked like she was thinking about it before she nodded. "Ok, I guess that could work. I don't know that they're going to be searching for pictures but..."

"And I have an appointment tomorrow with my tattoo guy." One that I scheduled on Thursday after my last appointment with him.

Mia took one step back but only so she could lean away from me. "You have an appointment with your tattoo guy?" she repeated, her voice down an octave and her chin dropping to accommodate. She was fucking cute as hell.

I nodded once. This was what I originally was going to tell her. "Yep." I popped the 'p' and nodded once more.

"You don't have any more room." She was looking at my sleeve where yeah, every inch of skin from just past my shoulder down to my wrist was covered in black and gray ink.

I held up that same arm and with my thumb, tapped the base of the finger between my pinky and middle fingers.

Mia frowned. "But that's…"

"Yep. That's right."

Her eyes widened. "It is *way* too soon to be talking about *marriage*, Conor!"

Sure, I thought the same thing, but I felt that kick in my heart. I covered up the disappointment, though. "Shit, I know that, Mia. But you're the mother of my kid—"

"People have kids and don't get married all the time!" Her voice was taking on that edge of panic she sometimes had. Her panic, and her words for the matter, was doing serious damage to my ego. As such, I couldn't manage to hold the pissed off tone from my voice.

"Are we back to that argument? You want out of this, Mia? Just do co-parenting and see each other when we pass the kid off?"

Her face fell but she was completely open, every emotion all over her face. "Well, no."

"Then let me fucking mark my damn ring finger for you. It's not a wedding band. But you're the mother of my kid, and I want you there."

Mia stared down at me for what felt like for-fucking-ever and finally she nodded with a shrug of her shoulder. Crazy woman with mixed gestures.

"Ok. All right, sure. Yeah."

"Good." There was definite satisfaction in my voice. Have I mentioned I'm a sore loser? Yeah, I liked to get my way. "Now, back to our previous programming." I winked up at her and stood, my body brushing against her belly and making her step back in the process. When I fully stood, I started to lift her dress all over again.

My eyes were fixed on her tits the entire time, fucking ecstatic to learn if she wore something lacy and fun on top too. You have to understand, my girl was a cotton panties and boring bra kind of gal. I tried to get her to buy a flowery print, in cotton even, at Target a few weeks ago, and she went with the regular white.

But she was wearing lace on her ass.

I needed to know if there was lace on her chest, too.

I nearly swallowed my fucking tongue, strangling Mia in the process because the dress was now up by her neck and head, when I saw what she had on.

My girl found herself a sexy side.

Shit, that sounded bad.

I found Mia sexy as all get out, strutting around with a baby belly that I gave her. She was smart, she was witty, she had class. But fucking A, her in lace was a sight to behold.

"Shit, Mia."

She wiggled and I shook my head, helping her out of her dress the rest of the way until she stood in front of me in just nude lace. The bra was unlined, unpadded, and I could see her dark areolas through the pattern.

Her smile was on the shy side, but her face was bright with happiness.   "I   did   good?"
"Fuck, yes, Mia. But it's gotta come off."

She took my hand and turned. "Bedroom."

And I followed her. Like a lovesick fool. But my cock and balls would be happy, and let's be honest, with this view? Mia walking in front of me, arm stretched back so she could lead me to my room, dressed in lace with crisscrossing straps between her shoulder blades? Fuck, she could take me anywhere.

CHAPTER THIRTEEN

MIA

I had been excited about playing with my toys with Conor back at my place, but splayed out on his huge bed was a pretty decent compromise.

That was the other thing. My toys. Conor wouldn't play with them with me during our month of no-sex, saying that playing, touching, was all considered sexual and he wanted complete abstinence. He wouldn't even let *me* play while he was around. Finding time to play with your toys while your, well, whatever Conor was –boyfriend?—wasn't around wasn't incredibly easy.

So tonight we'd be toyless which, let's be honest, would be completely fine. The man *looked* at me and I was wet. He put his hand on me and I was ready to shoot off into bliss.

I pulled Conor along to his bedroom, his hand squeezing mine. When we entered the room and I pulled us closer to the bed, Conor stopped and tugged me back into him, where he crossed an arm over the top of my chest and cradled my belly with his other arm.

"You're so fucking sexy," he whispered into my ear. I tilted my head to my shoulder, wordlessly asking him to press his lips to that magical spot. Smart man that he was, Conor complied, sucking, kissing, and nibbling up and down the column of my neck.

He slipped his hand under the top of my panties, holding his palm over my mound and his fingers just *sitting* on top of my folds. I spread my feet, trying to get his fingers to slip *into* the folds, to at least rest on top of my aching clit, but Conor seemed content in just holding me, kissing my neck, and holding his hand possessively over me.

"Conor." My voice came out a little whiny, and it was a bit embarrassing.

"Mia." His voice was barely a whisper in my ear. He turned me in his arms and leaned in to kiss me. As much as I actually enjoyed being pregnant, I would be happy when this bump wasn't between us. I wanted to be completely pressed up into Conor.

His beard scratched against my chin and I wound my hands loosely around his neck. His tongue slipped into my mouth and our kiss was heated but not frantic. I lifted my eyelids, needing to watch Conor, and wasn't at all surprised to see his hooded eyes fixed on mine.

He grinned boyishly against my lips as he pulled back. "God, I love you."

My heart stopped beating for a second, only to flutter rapidly against my ribs shortly after. I should say it was too soon. We didn't know each other.

But we did.

We spent a month getting to know one another again. He wasn't the Conor from my childhood, just as I was no longer the little kid who hung out at his house before he left for college. We were two different people and while I was probably a little too sweet for a guy like Conor, and he was probably a little too gruff and hard for a woman like me…

I liked who we were together.

So I whispered the three words into the air, feeling them with every piece of my being. "I love you too, Conor."

His grin was what fantasies were made of. Daily, he showed me how excited he was for this baby, and this grin right here told me how excited he was for us. Needing for us to be *more*, I reached between us and started to work on his pants.

"Naked, Conor," I said, drawing the zipper down.

I pushed down on the denim of his jeans, not at all surprised to see he'd gone commando, and before I could kneel to get the denim the rest of the way off, because hello, I couldn't bend at the waist these days, Conor put his hands over mine and finished the act for me.

"I can't have your mouth so close to me right now, Mia baby," was his gruff response and I couldn't help but grin. Someone was feeling needy.

After he straightened up, I had to chuckle at the sight he was. He was naked from the hips down, still sporting his bar tee on top. "You're cute."

Conor scoffed and peeled his shirt off over the top of his head. "That was fucking ass-backwards," he said, referring to the order in which he lost his clothes.

"Nah, it was good," I said, grinning. I reached out to trace the tattoo on his side. I knew the Gaelic knot he had on the back of his shoulder, and I had previously studied the lines and shapes of his sleeve, which had homages to his siblings and heritage intermixed, but these words were new.

"This is new." He must have gotten it sometime over the last few days.

He nodded, looking down to where my fingers traced. He lifted his arm a little to allow greater access. "Got it Thursday morning."

Which explained why it was still slightly red. Not badly, but just enough.

"What does it say?"

"*Dá fhada an lá tagann an tráthnóna.*"

The Gaelic lilt of his tongue was sexy and almost enough for me not to care what it meant. But, "Which means...?"

Apparently he was all about multitasking, because he dropped to his knees to peel my panties off, pressing a kiss to the underside of my belly, the top of my thigh, the top of my mound, all before answering, "'However long the day, the evening will come.'"

I lifted a brow. "You work nights, bud. Does that mean you don't like your days with me? You crave the bar at night?" I was grinning and there was a slight lift to my voice.

"No, smartass." He slapped my ass before standing and I stepped out of the lace pooled at my feet. "It means no matter how bad, no matter how long, the good will always come."

"Wow, Conor O'Gallagher has a philosophical side."

He just chuckled, shaking his head. "You really are a smartass." He reached behind me to undo the clasp of my bra, but when he did and the material didn't fall, the change in his face, from gleeful to confused, was comical.

"How the fuck does this come off?" Both of his hands went to my back to hold out the ends, but because it was a multi-way bra and I crisscrossed the straps...

"What, a man with your sexual prowess hasn't encountered a multi-way bra?"

"This a trick question?" His brows were down in concentration, but he still looked determined. "Over my head, cowboy."

I reached in front of me to pull the cups over my breasts, which spilled out when unconfined, and started to shimmy and twist it off over my head when Conor got with the program and finished the job.

"Finally," he said on an exasperated sigh, making me laugh. His hands went straight to my over-sized breasts and he kneaded them in his hands. "God, watching these get bigger and not being about to do anything with them..." He cut off his thought when he bent low to suck on one of my nipples. My head fell back at the feel of his mouth over me and I put my hands in his hair, keeping him pressed closed.

"God, Conor."

He chuckled against my flesh and when he ran his tongue over my now hardened peak, I damn near came. "Oh my God."

"Damn," he said, pulling away from my chest. "If I knew abstinence after a really good fuck would get you to start talking, I'd have done it sooner."

I lifted a brow. "Really, Conor? We had sex, didn't talk for five months, had sex nearly twice in one day, and then spent a month not touching. How much sooner do you think you should have planned to abstain?"

He grinned, then shrugged. "Should've gone with my gut when I was still thinking about you a week after the first time.

Should have found you. I could have figured it out."

"With what information?" I was trying not to, but I couldn't help but grin at his determination. "You didn't have my name, you knew nothing about me..."

"Stop being so smart about this, Mia." His grin was wide. "I should have figured out a way. Now stop talking. I want to feel you around me." He put his hand between my legs and flicked the tip of his finger over my clit, causing me to moan.

"Yeah, baby, just like that." He circled those fingers around the nub then strummed it back and forth before slipping his fingers further back. I fully expected him to sink two, if not three, fingers into me straight away, but he surprised me by starting with one.

"Gotta be sure you're ready," he said, watching my face as he moved his finger in and out slowly. "You're pretty fucking slick here, Mia baby."

"More," I said, grinding my hips against his hand.

"Ah, you're greedy today, yeah?" He pulled his finger out and went back to tormenting my clit.

I growled. Yes, I growled. "Conor."

"Tell me what you need." He lowered his mouth to my shoulder, where he pressed small kisses over and over again. His finger between my lower lips continued to play and he put his other hand on the side of my swollen belly. If I weren't so aroused, I would be smiling with happiness over the fact he always had a hand on my belly, but damn, I waited a long month for this night and I needed him.

"I need your cock, Conor. Your thick, freaking cock. I need you in me," I said, annoyed with him and so freaking turned on, I would surely burst the moment he filled my pussy with his cock.

Conor threw his head back with a short, loud laugh. "God*damn*, Mia."

"Well..." The shyness was back. I used my words like he asked me to, but maybe not in the exact way he wanted them.

He must have seen my face shut down because he put his lips to mine, kissing me deeply and thrusting two fingers into me. When my mouth opened, he took the opportunity to sweep his tongue into my mouth, kissing me thoroughly.

He continued to kiss me as his fingers thrusted in and out, scissoring inside me and curling against the walls. Faster and faster, he moved his hand until my legs felt like they were going to give out from under me.

I put my hands on his shoulders and pulled my mouth back, squeezing my eyes shut to focus on both the sensation happening between my legs, and on staying upright. Conor slide his free hand from my belly to my lower back, pressing me just enough to give me additional stability. He slipped a third finger inside my tight space and relentlessly moved his hand, faster now, and at an angle that allowed his palm to get my clit in on the action.

My jaw dropped open as the impending orgasm started. I could feel it coming and knew if I just squeezed against his fingers, adding just a little more tightness to the mix, I would fly over that edge.

I needed it, though.

So I did.

"Yeah, baby, take what you need," was Conor's response when I clamped down over his fingers. No sooner than the words were out of his mouth, and I was gone.

"Shit," I said as my body shook and shuddered against him. My chest was heaving and my legs were shaking. If it weren't for Conor's arms, I would be a puddle on the ground.

I opened my eyes as the true high finally finished, even with my body shuddering and the aftereffects of my orgasm still sending shockwaves of pleasure through my body.

"You're fucking beautiful." Conor slipped his hand from between my legs, his eyes fixed on the sight. As his eyes raked back up my body, they lingered on my chest. When they stayed there, I looked down as well.

"Oh my God!" I moved my hands to cover myself. I was *leaking*. Oh my God! Everyone always talked about how they had a baby and they were waiting for their milk to come in; what the fuck was this?

This was so embarrassing.

"Oh my God. I can't... Oh my..." I tried to step away, but Conor put his hands to my hips yet again, holding me in place.

Then, without a word, he did the one thing I never in my wildest dreams would have imagined, and quite frankly, had I thought of him doing it, I would have been mildly grossed out. He *licked* me.

"Conor!"

I tried to step back but he just moved to do the same to my other breast, his hands squeezing my hips.

"It's normal, Mia," he finally said as he straightened. "And oddly erotic."

"But... You... No! No, you can't do that. That's... *weird*, Conor."

He just grinned, his bearded cheeks lifting and this eyes twinkling in the dimming light of the room. "It's fucking hot." He turned me to face the bed and walked us right up to the edge before he covered my breasts with his hands, kneading them. "I read about it. Maybe watched a video or two, too."

I frowned, looking over my shoulder. "You read about it?" I hadn't even read about it! I pretty much just skimmed the 'what your baby looks like now' web pages and just, rolled with it all. But Conor was *reading* about my pregnancy? What universe was this?

"Yep. Read about it."

"And by watching, you mean..." I thought about it for a moment, then my eyes widened. I couldn't turn toward him because he was holding me in place but my jaw still dropped. "You watched *porn* about lactating women? Oh my God, Conor!"

He chuckled lightly. "I was curious about the fetish. Didn't quite get it. Even watching it, didn't really get it, but with you?" He nodded. "Totally get it."

"Do you watch porn regularly?" That could be a problem. Not a big problem, because it wasn't like I had never watched it, but if he was going to go that route instead of with me, that would be a problem.

"Mia. Babe. I just went a month without sex. Yeah, I watched it pretty regularly." His grin grew and he lifted a hand to swirl a finger in my face. "And you, miss, can't say a damn thing about it, because one of those times was on your laptop, and one of the sites was already archived."

I blushed even though it really wasn't anything to be super embarrassed about. The man knew I had toys so it shouldn't be that big of a deal but women and porn was just so... Taboo.

"I'd much rather be fucking you, though, if that's what you're worried about. But maybe someday we can watch together." He added his sexy wink and I decided to let it go. Because he had a point.

"Enough talk. You had your turn, it's mine." To prove his point, he held his body close to mine, his thick, hard cock trapped between our bodies and pushing into my back.

"How do you want me, then?" I was going with bravado tonight. He wanted me to be more vocal, I was going to certainly try.

"What do you think is going to be comfortable? You haven't been sleeping on your back." He *would* notice something like that.

I thought about it, trying to figure out which position would feel the best. When I stepped away from him this time he let me, and I crawled up on to his much-too-big bed, my belly hanging low, and grabbed a pillow to put under my chest. I lowered my upper body and looked back at him. "Good for you?"

His hand was on his cock, squeezing it and pumping from base to head. He licked his lower lip and his grin was wicked and visceral. He moved to kneel on the bed behind me, between my spread knees, and palmed my ass. "Damn, you're fucking gorgeous."

Putting his finger at the center and top of my ass, he lowered it slowly. My ass clenched when he ran over the bud there and I bit my lip when he rimmed my pussy opening. I was still soaked from earlier, more than ready for his thick girth.

His finger left me and, glancing over my shoulder again, I saw him take himself in hand, moving even closer. He swept the head of his cock over the path his finger just took and ran his other hand up my back, reaching up to clasp around the back of my neck. He squeezed once gently just before he pushed in fully.

My head dropped to my crossed forearms, my mouth open on the soundless plea his entering me always seemed to provoke. With his arm at my neck and his cock deep inside me, his body blanketed mine gently. He dropped his other hand to rest on knuckles beside me, giving me the feeling of being completely enveloped without his body weight directly on me.

"Goddamn, I missed this," he grunted as he pulled out slowly. He squeezed my neck once more before moving that hand to mirror his other, allowing him to press kisses up and down my spine as he started to work his hips against mine.

Wantonly, I pushed back against him every time he thrust, needing him deeper and harder than he was already going.

"More, Conor."

He chuckled against my back before pushing himself up straight, his hands at my hips. If anything, he slowed his thrusts down, letting his pull drag deliciously against my inner walls.

"Oh my God, Conor." I moved my arms so they were beside me in push-up position, only so I could keep my open mouth gasp muffled against his mattress. He pulled back and cocked his hips, twisted the angle enough to cause small moans of ecstasy to crash through my mouth. I didn't feel him move a hand from my hip, but soon my hair was being pulled gently, enough to take my mouth from his bed, my head back and neck exposed.

"I want to hear it, Mia. Tell me what this does to you. Tell me what my thick cock in this tight pussy does to you."

"God, Conor, it's fucking..." I moaned again, my eyes closed. "Right there, Conor. Right there." I pushed back onto him, which earned me a chuckle and slight swat to my ass.

"Tell me, don't take, Mia baby."

"Harder, Conor."

"Like this?" He let go of my hair and gripped my hips with both hands again, slamming hard up into me.

"Oh God, Yes, Conor." The feel of his thickness inside me, the slick and quick push past my muscles, had me incredibly close to coming again.

He did it one more time, but I needed more. "Faster, Conor.

Fuck me like you want me."

He held himself in me so incredibly deep and didn't move. "Don't ever think I don't want you, Mia baby. Fuck, I want you. I fucking need you."

Before I could respond though, his hips were pounding into me ruthlessly, giving me everything I needed and more. I muttered his name over and over, mixed in with high moans and senseless words, squeezing my eyes shut against the onslaught of feeling.

I was so close.

So damn close.

Knowing, God he knew me so fucking well, Conor reached around me and held his finger over my clit, our rocking hips causing his finger to move ever so slightly.

But just enough to send me over.

"Oh, fuck, Conor!" Rather than bury my head in the mattress, I threw my head back, my arms and neck straining with my release.

"Yeah, baby. Just like that." His hips continued to work against me, his thick cock pushing against the resistance my orgasm was causing until finally his loud grunt matched my quiet mews of pleasure.

And then it was over too soon.

Conor pulled out and I moaned at the loss. Rather than him leave to clean himself up though, he lay beside me, pulling me onto my side yet facing away from him. He then pulled me close and wrapped his arm around me, his hand resting on my belly gently and kissed my shoulder.

Here we were in this huge bed, and he wanted to keep me close. I couldn't stop the onslaught of tears from filling my eyes, even though it was a stupid thing to get teary about.

I closed my eyes, hoping Conor wouldn't notice, but the damn man seemed to notice everything.

"What's wrong?" I felt him push up behind me so he could look into my face.

"Nothing, I'm fine," I said, not really lying. I put my hands under my cheek and tried to settle in for a nap. I winced when the baby chose that moment to kick something vital but I kept my eyes closed.

For a second, I thought Conor was going to drop it but instead he climbed over me. I opened my eyes, which of course caused a tear to spill, and saw him sitting on his knees, looking down at me. The sight was actually quite comical, big burly, bearded, tatted man sitting on his knees while naked, looking down at me.

"Ah, I knew it!" He pointed at my face but then his own face fell. "Why are you crying, Mia?"

"It's stupid," I said, while trying to grin. "They're not sad tears, I promise."

Conor moved so he was lying down on his side, facing me this time, but kept his upper body propped up on his arm. He brushed a finger down my cheek, tracking a tear.

"What's wrong, Mia baby?" he asked quietly.

"I was just thinking about how you have this huge bed and you choose to stay wrapped up close to me. See? Stupid. Nothing for you to worry about."

He ran his thumb over my cheek and grinned crookedly. "Yeah, well, I told you. I like your bed. This fucker's too big for the two of us."

"I like your bed though." It turned out I enjoyed cuddling, but I was sure there would come a day that we would need our space in bed.

"And I like yours. You lose this argument, Mia." He relaxed his arm and lay down fully beside me, his eyes just taking in my face and features. I nearly wiggled from the uncomfortable perusal, but I refrained.

Finally, after a few quiet moments, Conor spoke up. "We have to talk baby things soon."

CHAPTER FOURTEEN

CONOR

I may have only had sex with Mia a handful of times, if even—but hey, it was still more than I could say I did with any other individual woman—but I knew without a single doubt that this woman, wrapped in my arms, was who I wanted to be with for the next fifty-plus years.

The sex just got better and better. Each time, Mia vocalized what she needed and wanted a little more, which only turned me the fuck on more.

But tears in her eyes afterward? I was not prepared for that.

Then when she gave the line about the bed, I wanted to laugh out loud. She was crying because I had a huge ass mother fucking bed and I wanted to keep her close instead.

Depending on how many kids we'd have, yeah, maybe we'd get a bigger bed than her queen someday. You know, to accommodate bad dreams and stuffed animals, but I was absolutely content with her smaller mattress.

Which brought up the point, where were we putting the bed?

Her place didn't even have a fucking separate *room* to put the baby, and my place, even though it had rooms unlike her studio, wasn't exactly prime real estate for a baby. Not above a bar, and not with a room the baby could someday call its own.

Then there was the fact we didn't have a name yet. I was cool with the whole not finding out the sex thing, but the kid needed a name.

"We need to talk baby things soon," I finally said out loud.

"What do you mean?" she asked. I reached down to

maneuver the covers around us and as much as I wanted to have her pressed as close as her back to me allowed, I needed her face and eyes more. I moved so my abs pressed against her belly, grinning when the kid kicked or pushed or whatever it did, and Mia entwined our legs together.

"Names. Where we're going to live. Those things."

"Oh." She nodded a few times as if thinking. "I don't think living here is that great of an idea, to be honest."

I agreed, but wanted to hear her reasoning. "Ok. Why?"

She lifted her brows and moved to sit up, pushing against the bed and moving to allow her belly space. I loved watching as her movements changed to make way for her belly.

I moved to my back and pushed back so I could rest against the headboard, watching her. I crossed my arms over my chest and waited for what she had to say, loving the fact that she didn't bother to pull the sheet with her to cover her tits.

"Well first, it's over a bar. Not exactly a great environment for a child. As an infant, it wouldn't be bad, but I don't think it would be so great with a toddler." She shrugged. "I have no problem with the baby hanging around downstairs while you're opening and whatever, but definitely not anywhere near the place when it starts to get busy."

"I agree." I didn't think she was expecting me to agree so easily.

"O-kay..."

Nope. She definitely didn't think I'd agree so quickly.

"Well, also, there's not really room for the baby. Like, there's not a physical room for it."

Again, I agreed, but just to be a fucker... "I could always frame out another room, take away some square footage from this room and the closet."

She thought about it, her eyes scanning the room as she pondered that. "Yeah..." She nodded in that thoughtful way of hers. "Yeah, I guess that could work."

She continued to look around the room before pointing to the door to my room. "You probably had some woman right there against the door."

I grinned. I hadn't thought about that, but yeah, she would go there.

"And probably in your bathroom, too. Not to mention the kitchen, the couch. Hell, you probably even got some on the stairs leading up here."

I chuckled. "I get it. You don't want to live where I had my...looser ways."

She frowned. "Is that bad of me? I mean, I know you swear you're a changed man, and I really do believe you, but for me personally, the reminder is all over."

I reached for her, pulling her by her neck until she crawled to sit right next to me. "I was thinking about finding an apartment or a house with you. I just wanted to hear what you had to say."

"You want to move in together?"

I barked out a laugh. "Mia. We practically live together already, just without the change of address form."

Mia smiled wide. "Ok. Yeah. Maybe tomorrow after my appointment, we can start looking? Do you have to do book work tomorrow?"

I was about to shake my head, because I had been intending to get that done, but remembered I fell asleep before I could. I made a face and nodded, "Yeah, but it can wait until after everything."

Again, Mia smiled. "Ok. Sounds like a plan then."

MIA

The next day, everything happened quickly. Conor had woken me up a number of times through the night, to 'play', as he called it, and we finally got out of bed with an hour to spare before my appointment.

The appointment itself went smoothly, with my OB-GYN just asking about birth plan things and asking Conor how he felt about everything. She also wanted to see the baby's position, saying that in a few weeks' time, the baby would be in what should be its final position for birth. She had concerns of the baby potentially being breech.

She ordered a quick ultrasound to check, and if Conor and I had been hopeful about not finding out the baby's sex, well...

Our baby had other ideas.

The moment the wand was placed on my belly, our baby was all about showing what it was.

Conor laughed out loud. "That baby is all boy."

My doctor smiled. "I know you wanted to wait. I'm sorry, Mia. But yes, like Conor said, your baby is definitely all boy."

"Look at him. He's showing off."

"Like his dad," I said, when I finally found my voice. My eyes were tearing up and when Conor looked at me, I was afraid he was going to think I was crying because I was disappointed. I held my hand up and shook my head. "I'm fine. Overwhelmed, but really, really happy."

Conor leaned in and kissed my lips sweetly as my doctor started to clean up her equipment. "Well, I can say that I think he will be fine. We'll keep an eye on him, because he is getting pretty big and is going to run out of room, but everything looks good."

I smiled and thanked her, and after she left with brief instructions on what to do in the coming weeks, Conor pulled my shirt down and helped me stand.

"You're really ok?" he asked.

I nodded. "I am. Yeah, I wanted it to be a surprise, you know, the last great surprise a person could get, but..." I shrugged and grinned, shaking my head. "He's going to be such a little hellion."

"Just like his old man."

I reached up on tiptoes so I could kiss him once. I wanted a long, thorough kiss, but my OB-GYN's room was so not the place.

"Let's go look at places to live so I can take you home and ravish you senseless." Conor squeezed my hip and grabbed my purse, not afraid to put the strap over his shoulder, and helped me out of the room.

That day, we toured two nicer apartments and, after Conor's urging, a little starter house located on a cute cul-de-sac. An apartment was a one-year commitment. A house? That was a serious commitment, as both a homeowner and for a new couple.

On top of that, I was afraid a mortgage was going to put us over our heads, but Conor assured me we could afford it.

We.

He referred to us as a 'we' and while I knew he said he was in for the long haul, it was those little reminders that made my heart so incredibly happy.

It was a three bedroom, two bath ranch-style home with a small yard, but the neighborhood itself had a little park. Conor said we could convert the third bedroom into an office for now, allowing him to work from home even more.

So finally, a smile on my face, I nodded. "Ok. Let's do the paperwork."

And we started the next adventure in our life.

EPILOGUE

MIA

Conor was running late again. Saturday afternoons always had him walking in the door almost two hours after the end of his shift, but I knew the man only had eyes for me. That and I knew he tried to get as much Sunday paperwork finished before he came home, preferring to focus on us when he was home. After talking with Brenna, I found myself at O'Gallaghers.

The place was crazy busy and a glance at the bar itself told me why. The Enforcers were starting to trickle into town. According to Conor, camp was opening up this week and apparently the veterans of the team were having a bonding day.

I had gotten to know a few of the players, but it was easy to spot Jonny and Caleb Prescott. Jonny, with his curly blond hair, and Caleb beside him.

I waddled over to them, my baby belly bigger than ever, and squeezed between the brothers, tapping them on their shoulders. "Hello, gentlemen."

Jonny looked over at me and grinned as he lifted his beer to his lips. "Miss Mia."

Caleb grinned at me as well. "Look at you, all glowing and shit."

I grinned wide. "How's Sydney? I haven't seen her in a bit." After the wedding, and after things started to settle into a sweet, regular motion with me and Conor, I grew to be good friends with Sydney Prescott. She was a fun girl.

Before Caleb could answer though, Conor came over to us. He started switching out his O'Gallagher shirts for shirts that showcased he was taken. Today's said, boldly over his chest, "I

Make Cute Babies." Today he also wore a backward ball cap with a bumble bee over his brow. I knew the front of that hat said "Daddy to Bee". It was a favorite of his and honestly, made me laugh.

"What the hell are you doing here, Mia baby?" He was grinning wide, absolutely no malice in his voice. "You know I don't want you here when you're ready to pop like that."

I grinned and rubbed my belly. "I was just curious why you weren't home. I now understand why."

He glanced over his shoulder. I followed his gaze and saw he was looking at the clock, but my eyes landed on the pictures he placed there. He wasn't shy about showing he was taken and happy about it.

There was also the fancy 'm' on his ring finger, silly man.

"Shit. Sorry, babe." He looked back around and pulled his towel from his pocket. "Stone, man, I gotta fly."

"Conor..." It really wasn't that pressing.

"I got a date with my baby mama."

This earned a chuckle from not only the Prescotts, but a few of the other players nearby.

"Jeez, Conor." I could feel my face heating.

He winked at me and crooked his finger at me. I followed him to the end of the bar, where he took my hand and pulled me into the back. "Hey, I could have said I had a date to fuck the labor out of you."

I slapped his back. "Conor!" He had said it in what was supposed to be an empty kitchen, but Rory came out of the stairwell from the upstairs apartment. We got the house, and Rory took over upstairs.

"Way too much fucking information," Rory said, shaking his shaggy head.

"I'm a lucky fuck, you know it," Conor said with a laugh, pulling me into his office. He clicked the door shut, locking it twice, because *there* was a story, and pulled me to the couch.

He tore his hat off with one hand while removing his shirt with his other, behind his back and over his head in the way men did, and unfastened his jeans. "You wearing panties today?"

I was wearing a dress, and going panty-less wasn't exactly the most comfortable but, "No, I am not." We had limited time these days.

"How long did Brenna—" Conor had added a really nice leather couch to the office here at the bar recently, one that was deep and gave the two of us more than enough room. He sat down and pulled me to him. I lifted a leg over his hips as he laid back, settling down over him, my wet heat rubbing over his thickness. I rolled my hips once, dragging myself over his rigid length.

"An hour."

Conor leaned up to kiss me, guiding my hips until he slipped into my warmth. We moaned in unison.

The last few weeks hadn't been very kind to my sex drive, but I was ready for this baby to come out. Labor-inducing sex, it was then.

It was over quicker than we usually went, but that was due to going weeks without sex, and the contractions toward the end.

Holding his hands over my sides, feeling the contractions for himself, Conor looked up at me, his eyes a mixture of glee and worry.

"Is it time?"

I laughed. I really didn't think one session was going to do it. "Nah, I think they're just Braxton hicks. She's pretty comfy-cozy in there." I groaned when she kicked. "She's probably never going to come out."

If I thought I was huge with Aiden, I was not prepared for this pregnancy. With Ava, I felt her up in my ribs all the time, and my belly needed a Wide Load sign.

I pushed up onto my knees, allowing Conor to slip from my heat, and with my hands against his chest, moved to stand.

Conor sat up and looked at the clock. "Bren has Aiden for another thirty minutes. Want to get food?" He reached for his clothes and started to pull them back on as I reached for a tissue to try to clean up as best as I could.

Which was hardly at all.

Conor chuckled and reached for my hand, taking the tissue and going to task, before finishing dressing.

The past few months had been a whirlwind. Aiden Rory O'Gallagher was born, weighing in at ten pounds, eleven ounces, and twenty-two inches. He was *big*. And because of that, I tore pretty decently.

Conor had been a hands-on dad the moment we walked into our little house on the cute cul-de-sac, and had been incredibly great at making sure I stayed comfortable. I tried breast feeding, because goodness knew I had the supply for it, but Aiden hadn't been a great latcher, and after a week of trying and therefore crying, I moved to just pumping and bottle feeding. It allowed Conor to feed him too, and there was nothing I loved more than to watch Conor and Aiden together.

After two months of pumping though, we had more than enough milk to get Aiden to his one-year birthday. I was a super-cow, I joked, to which of course Conor took offense to.

The whole calling myself a cow thing.

Anyway. I stopped pumping pretty early in the game.

Conor had been afraid of 'down there'. Not because I gave birth. No, it was because I tore so badly. He was afraid he would hurt me or worse, I would somehow just randomly tear again. One day we'd been messing around, not having sex yet because regardless of Conor's fears, we still didn't have the medical go-ahead, and Conor jacked off on me.

A month later, while doing my yearly blood panel for insurance purposes, boom. Pregnant.

I'm not making this stuff up.

So our kids were going to be hardly ten months apart. When I told Conor the news, his face blanched so quickly, I thought that my big man was going to faint on me.

He then called my OB-GYN to be sure that everything was going to be ok, that *I* was going to be ok. She reassured him, saying that it definitely wasn't the best thing for my *body*, but I should have a normal pregnancy. She just was going to keep a closer eye on me.

As we left his office hand in hand, Conor said his goodbyes to his brother and Stone, and the few hockey players still lingering around the bar. We went to my car, leaving his new truck in the back lot. Conor helped me in before going around to the driver's side.

"Grab something and head home, or ask Bren to stay a little longer and sit down somewhere?" Conor asked as he started the ignition.

We didn't have too much time to ourselves these days. Hard to with a nine and a half month old at home who was sure to skip the walking stage and go straight from crawling to running.

But I also hated being away from Aiden. Going back to work had been incredibly hard, but I was lucky to be able to spend weekends and summers with him.

"Maybe just pick something up. Brenna said she had plans later tonight."

"With a guy?" Conor looked at me, a brow up, and I grinned.

"Even if she were going on a date, it would be of no business of yours, Conor."

"Hey, she's my baby sister."

"And she's a grown woman."

Brenna and I had gotten incredibly close over the last year, too. We were obviously two very different people than we were when we were friends before, but I definitely valued her friendship.

"Speaking of grown women... I talked to your dad."

I whipped my head in his direction. "You didn't."

Conor had been teasingly threatening to talk to my dad about taking my hand in marriage. Conor wanted me to marry him, and as much as I wanted to marry him too, as much as he'd proven himself over and over again these last few months, I still felt like everything was too fast.

Sure, we were on our way to having two kids, but marriage...? That was a really, *really* big step. I mean, kids were a big step; they linked him to me for the rest of our lives. But something about marriage scared me a little.

"I told him that eventually you would be ok with the idea,

and that I wanted to be sure I had his permission." Conor reached for my hand and squeezed it before placing our hands on his thigh. "I got it. So I'm just waiting on you, baby." He said it with a grin. Conor was so incredibly supportive of me and I could tell he loved me above all else. "Whenever you're ready, I'll be right there with you," he said, pulling our hands to his lips to kiss my knuckles.

He was really a great guy.

Great in bed, too, yes, but his heart and how he was with me, with Aiden, that was what kept me going day after day.

"I love you, Conor," I finally said. No, I wasn't ready for marriage, but soon. Definitely, soon.

"Love you too, Mia baby."

Did you enjoy Brenna and Stone's story?
Please consider leaving a review on Amazon!
Also, be sure to check out the Troublemakers: Mignon Mykel's
reader group on Facebook!

Continue reading for a look at
Interference—Caleb and Sydney's story!

INTERFERENCE

CALEB

I shouldn't have gone to O'Gallaghers with Jonny last night.

I pulled my pillow from under my head and, face planting into the mattress, pushed the sides as close to my ears as possible. Anything to block out the annoying ring of my cell phone.

Last night, San Diego won. As was tradition, Jon Jon and I went out on the town. Sometimes the other guys on the team would come along but for the most part, it was just me and the kid brother. Back in our peewee hockey days, mom would take us to McDonald's; in college, the one year he and I attended at the same time, we would party in my dorm. Now, we went out, partied long and hard, and of course, shut it down. Most of the bartenders looked the other way with some of the younger athletes in town, and we could always count on Conor O'Gallagher. Rumor had it the O'Gallaghers were a little rough around the edges. Probably why Conor was willing to overlook Jonny not quite being twenty-one yet.

Both Jonny and I had been drafted to the San Diego Enforcers. During my senior year of college, Jonny's freshman year, we both walked into training camp as college kids with great stats, and walked out with spots on the roster. Sure, the Prescott name means something to the organization, but Jonny was a damn good goaltender, and my stats were better than dad's in the respect he didn't touch majors until he was in his mid-twenties, having played in the American league for a few years beforehand.

Last night's win meant the Enforcers were that much closer

to Sir Stanley and his Cup. Finals were well within our reach. All we had to do was win Tuesday night's game and we'd make it into the next round. It was a close series, but the odds were in our favor. With Jonny in net, Vegas had to pull all the punches to get the puck past him.

I sighed blissfully when my phone finally stopped ringing, but just as I was about to drop off that sharp edge of sleep, Jonny slammed my bedroom door open. I lifted the pillow enough to look over my shoulder at the intrusion, watching as my boxer-clad brother tossed the cordless house phone onto my bed, bouncing off my hamstring–a little too close for comfort.

"Fucking asshole."

Jonny merely raised a dark blond brow. Oh, the perks of sharing a condo with your younger brother.

I guess it could be worse. My sisters weren't exactly the easiest to live with.

"Next time, wake up and answer your damn phone," Jonny grumbled. "There's a lady on the other end, and I don't think she much appreciated my sarcasm."

I reached back for the phone with one hand as I tossed the pillow aside with the other, before shooting Jonny the bird. As I put the phone to my ear, I watched my twenty-year old brother shuffle back toward his own room. "Caleb," I said on the exhale of a tired sigh.

"Um, hi," came the voice on the other end. Female, like Jonny said. Not high pitched, but not as sexy and throaty as some female voices were. Nervous, maybe. I didn't think I knew her voice, and the landline number was pretty locked down, so she couldn't be some weird stalker chick. I squeezed my eyes shut briefly. Way too much thinking for this hour.

"I'm so sorry that this seems to be an inopportune time. I figured you'd be up and moving, as it's ten." Was it ten already? "I thought that was the time you started practice on game days. I'm on a tight deadline and was really hoping to just leave a message." Ah, she didn't expect to actually talk to me.

"And this is..." I stated, not asked, before yawning.

"I'm sorry," she apologized again. "My name is Sydney Meadows and I'm calling on behalf of Sorenson Media Group. I tried to reach you through your agent, but he directed me straight to you."

I made a mental note to talk to Mark the first chance I got. He really needed to stop directing people to me. Wasn't that his job? To figure out what appearances and gigs were best for his athletes when they weren't doing what they were being paid to do? Fuck, Mark knew I didn't like to sign up for the extra things that came with being a pro-athlete. Events with the team, sure. Gigs at the rink, absolutely. But beyond that, it was a hard no.

"We are putting together a reality television series, and you are one of the names we were interested in having involved with the show," she stated in a rehearsed manner.

I didn't think sleep was going be coming back to me anytime soon, so I rolled over onto my back before throwing my legs over the side of the bed. As I stood, I shook my head. "Yeah, sorry. No reality TV."

"If you'd just let me pitch it to you—"

"That's all you're going to be doing, Miss Meadows. Do you really want to waste your breath? I'm not doing television."

"That's fine," she rushed to say. As she began talking about multiple women and just as many dates, I strode naked to my dresser to pull out a pair of old, worn sweatpants. I pulled them on while listening with one ear. She continued to talk, so I continued to move, walking out of my room and down the hall that was home to both mine and Jonny's rooms, a spare room, and a bathroom, before walking barefooted down the stairs. Whenever she'd pause for an answer, I was sure to give a barely verbal 'mmhm' just so she would continue her rant and be closer to done.

I had sisters. I knew how to work a phone call with the long-winded female species.

"So great," she said finally, with a smile evident in her voice, so unlike the unsure tone at the beginning of our conversation, one-sided as it mostly was. "I will meet you tonight after your game. Thank you so much, Caleb. I promise you, you won't be disappointed."

Standing in front of the fridge now, I frowned when I heard

the telltale sign of her ending the call. I pulled the phone from my ear only to stare down at the 'call ended' screen, the frown not going anywhere.

Well shit...

What did I just agree to?

AVAILABLE NOW!

ABOUT MIGNON MYKEL

Mignon Mykel is the author of the Love In All Places series. When not sitting at Starbucks writing whatever her characters tell her to, you can find her hiking in the mountains of Arizona. Mignon writes in one world, so while every series can be read as a standalone, her stories will be more enjoyable if you read them in publication order.

* *The Playmaker Duet (Troublemaker, Breakaway, Altercation, Holding)
can be enjoyed in one easy boxed set.*

Made in the USA
Middletown, DE
22 April 2021

38207681R00083